Mandy Baggot lives in leafy Wiltshire and has Sting as a neighbour. She lives with her husband, two daughters and two cats (Kravitz and Springsteen). When she isn't writing she loves to sing and do Lady Gaga impressions (check out You Tube).

In 2012, Mandy won the Innovation in Romantic Fiction award at the UK's Festival of Romance. Her novel Strings Attached was also short listed for the Best Author Published Read.

Praise for Mandy Baggot

I've just read your book and thought it was excellent! It had a real 'feel good' factor about it. (Excess All Areas)

I was entertained by the book from beginning to end and when I finished reading it, I felt the same satisfied feeling I have after watching a good film. (Breaking the Ice)

The book takes a thorough look at relationships, love, commitment and honesty and all the complicated baggage that comes with the territory. It is chick-lit to its fingertips! (Knowing Me Knowing You)

Public Property

Mandy Baggot

Published in 2013 by CreateSpace

Copyright © Mandy Baggot

First Edition

The author asserts the moral right under the Copyright, Designs and Patents Act 1988 to be identified as the author of this work. All Rights reserved. No part of this publication may be reproduced, stored in a retrieval system, or transmitted, in any form or by any means without the
prior written consent of the publisher, nor be otherwise circulated in any form of binding or cover other than that in which it is published and without a similar condition being imposed on the subsequent purchaser.

All characters and events in this publication, other than those clearly in the public domain, are fictitious and any resemblance to real persons, living or dead, is purely coincidental.

British Library C.I.P.

A CIP catalogue record for this title is available from the British Library.

One

Where were her pants? It was Wednesday and 'Wild Wednesday' pants had a picture of a cowgirl waving a lasso on the front of them. Freya Johnson rifled through the top drawer of the wooden dresser, continuing the search. She had found 'Sexy Sunday' and 'Funky Friday' but no 'Wild Wednesday'. She really didn't have time for this pants dilemma today. She sighed, gave up the search and opted for a plain black pair.

'Hey, is it not "Wild Wednesday"?' her fiancé, Nicholas Kaden remarked. He entered their bedroom and playfully hit her behind with the towel he had been using to dry his hair. He was fresh from the shower and still wet. Freya licked her lips and then restored the frown to her face.

'Have you seen them? Has Willis been through my knicker drawer again?'

Willis was their black and white cat. He liked weird stuff.

'Hmm, maybe. Did you never think that Willis and I might be in league together? A pact to ensure you're panty-less for longer?' Nicholas asked her. He was grinning. Here they called it a 'shit-eating' grin. Back in the UK she'd called it a smug-arse-face. He still managed to look gorgeous.

'I could believe that of you but not of sweet little Willis,' Freya responded as she put a cream short-sleeved top over her head and picked up a pair of black trousers from the floor.

'*Sweet* little Willis? The same cat who, when he isn't doing his business in my shoes, is scratching the hell out of the sofa,' Nicholas reminded her as he continued to dry himself off.

'He's just adjusting, you know, marking his territory. A bit like we did when we first arrived here,' Freya spoke, smiling. They'd just about marked every room. In fact they'd broken the coffee table.

'I don't remember crapping in anyone's shoes.'

'You really don't remember the house-warming party, do you?' Freya said, running a brush through her blonde hair and checking her reflection in the mirror.

'I remember you trying to get all our neighbours to play drinking games with you.'

'But it wasn't *me* who suggested playing naked "Twister". That was Brian and he's not going to be invited to the next gathering.'

Nicholas laughed.

'I've got Sadie Fox coming to see me today,' Freya told him as she began to search around the bedroom for her shoes.

'For a shoot?'

'No, not yet. She wants to talk first, tell me in great detail how she likes things done. How did she put it? *What she expects from her photographers*,' Freya replied.

'Yeah well, don't let her boss you around. She isn't the only fashion designer interested in your work. You're good and if she doesn't realise then it's her loss,' Nicholas said. He chose a shirt from the wardrobe.

'Boss me around? Do you really think she could?' Freya questioned, finding one of her shoes under the bed.

'No, I guess you're right, forget I said anything.'

'So, what are you doing today? Another day sat on the sofa calling it work?' Freya asked him.

'Hey, it *is* working. I was reading through a script,' he reminded her.

'*Hey it is working, I was reading through a script.* Who are you trying to kid? Sitting watching the Hallmark channel with a jug of lemonade and a plate of nachos is not working,' Freya said, laughing.

'You're just jealous,' Nicholas said. He smiled, a nice one, not the smug-arse-face.

'Yes I am.'

'Well, this morning I'm going to see Mark Phillips about the autobiography. Then I was planning to go for a run because last night someone persuaded me to take a shower with them, instead of working out. I'll need to do double today. Then I was going to sit and watch the Hallmark channel and read through the script,' he said.

'Is sex not a work out?' Freya asked him, a grin on her face.

'Last night probably was,' he admitted, nodding.

'So, you're still undecided about the film then," Freya said, locating her other shoe under a pile of towels on the floor.

'Yeah, still undecided.'

Freya watched him pull on a pair of blue jeans. It was little times like these she thanked the Lord for him.

'How much sex, violence and foul language in the script?' she asked.

'Um minimal sex, a couple of F-words, but a reasonable amount of violence.'

'I'm surprised they haven't upped the nudity, seeing as you aren't opposed to getting it all out on camera,' Freya said, giggling.

'I don't get it out for just anyone you know,' he insisted.

'No?' she asked, moving across the room towards him.

'No.'

'Well, I think you should go back to them and say you want at least ten more butt scenes. That would be what I'd want out of a movie,' Freya told him.

She stopped him from buttoning up his shirt and smoothed her hands over his stomach, moving them up to his chest.

'It would, would it?' he responded, pulling her top upwards.

'Hmm...and...maybe not!'

She let him go and bounded out of the bedroom.

'Hey! Come back here! There are names for women like you,' Nicholas called out, chasing her onto the landing.

Freya screamed and hurried down the stairs, heading for the kitchen.

'Come here, you tease,' he ordered as he followed her, at speed, around the breakfast bar and back out of the kitchen, down the hallway towards the front door.

'Stop right there or I open the front door. It's freezing and Donny's there *and* Kevin and two other faces I don't recognise,' Freya threatened, referring to the photographers outside their home.

'I'm not the one who's going to have my clothes ripped off,' Nicholas warned, pushing her against the door and kissing her neck.

'Unbolting the door right now. It's going to be the centre spread in *Shooting Stars* magazine,' Freya said, reaching up to pull the chain off the door latch.

'OK, OK, you win,' Nicholas conceded, stepping back from her with a sigh.

'I'm sorry. I'd love nothing more than to have you out of those jeans, but I can't be late this morning,' Freya reminded him.

'I know, I know, it's Sadie Fox. And no matter what a tyrant she is, I know you would love to photograph for her,' Nicholas replied.

'Think of the money we could give to charity. She seriously over pays.'

'I know, you said, it's fine. You can leave me frustrated, I'll deal,' Nicholas answered, kissing her cheek.

'I'll make it up to you. Listen, there's leftover pizza if you want breakfast. I'm going to have to dash,' Freya said, looking at her watch.

'Without even a cup of tea?' He raised an eyebrow.

'Oh I've had a cup of tea and I've fed Willis and the photographers have had tea too. And I did all that while I was trying to find my Wednesday pants,' Freya informed him with a smile.

'You are one amazing woman,' Nicholas told her.

'And don't you forget it. Speaking of not forgetting things…you have remembered we're going to Sam and Jolie's tonight for Sam's birthday, haven't you?' Freya asked. She took her handbag from where it hung over the banister.

'Is that tonight?'

'You mean the efficient Sandra hasn't emailed you your schedule yet? Yes, it's tonight so could you drop into Masons and pick up the fancy dress outfits on your way through?' Freya asked him.

'Fancy dress? You mean costumes?'

'Yes, costumes. Wait until you see what you're wearing,' Freya said with a laugh.

'I'm dreading it already.'

'OK, well, wish me luck with the viper-tongued fashion designer,' Freya said, taking her car keys from her handbag.

'Good luck and call me. Let me know how it goes,' he said.

'Don't forget, extra nudity in that script and, hold that thought until later,' Freya said. Her suggestion was clear.

'I certainly will.' He kissed her lips.

'Bye,' Freya said. She opened the door.

'Bye,' Nicholas replied.

Freya stepped out onto the wooden porch and sucked in a breath. Winter wasn't a favourite season of hers and the past month it had been uncharacteristically cold. The next week threatened to bring snow and she knew the kind of snow they got in the US wasn't the light dusting usually experienced in the UK. Nick had mentioned chains and snow shoes and bulky clothes. The only good thing was snow meant Christmas had to be getting closer. She loved Christmas!

As she left the house the photographers began to take pictures. It was one of the downsides of living with a Hollywood actor. However, she had found that by taking them an early morning cup of tea, dressed only in a nightshirt and robe, all other photographs they took were infinitely better. And once people had seen one photograph of her in her night clothes they weren't really interested in another. Besides, she didn't feel duty bound to protect her image like Nicholas did.

'Boys, is it really necessary? You've had me in my Mickey Mouse pyjamas this morning. And they weren't even my best pair,' Freya called to them as she walked down the steps towards her car.

'But they were very nice. I liked the ribbons,' Donny, one of the photographers called back to her.

'Hey Donny, if you want raw photos I'd stick around because Nick's dressing up tonight,' Freya informed him.

'Will there be left over takeout?'

'Don't push it.'

She got into her red Ford Expedition and shut the door behind her. How her life had changed.

In the space of a year she had met Nicholas Kaden, become engaged, sold her photography business in England and moved to America. She smiled as she remembered the impromptu holiday to Corfu to visit her best friend Emma – that break had changed everything.

Emma's life had been altered forever too. She was now a wife and mother and little Melissa Susan Petroholis - two months old - was making her presence felt in the world, usually in the early hours of the morning.

But that holiday had been important for another reason. It had helped Freya leave her life as Jane Lawson-Peck completely behind. Her father, Eric Lawson-Peck was a billionaire business man with companies all over the world and fingers in lots of pies. But he was also a monster. He had beaten Freya throughout her childhood and his treatment, coupled with the extravagant way her parents had led their lives, had culminated in Freya spending nine months in jail after setting fire to their home. She had been just eighteen.

Thankfully, that nightmare was now all in the past. Nicholas knew everything and accepted her for who she was. He also accepted her for the size she was.

Freya's weight had always been a battle and a battle she really wasn't interested in fighting. She loved food, she hated exercise. It was a lethal combination. She was a size twenty. She sometimes lost a few pounds, sometimes gained a few pounds but ordinarily she stuck and that was her. Take it or leave it. She knew she wouldn't be able to change and she was getting towards feeling comfortable with that.

Despite being devastatingly handsome, Nicholas had certain confidence issues too. He had beaten testicular cancer some years previously but had only felt able to share this information with the world after he met Freya. She had given him the strength to go public and, since broadcasting the news, they had set up the Nicholas Kaden Foundation. It raised money towards cancer research and bought vital equipment to assist in diagnosis and treatment.

Freya started up the car and drove down the gravel driveway towards the photographers at the gate. They moved out of the way as the electronic gate swung open and she waved at them as she headed off up the road.

Now home for Nicholas and Freya was Mayleaf, a small town on the outskirts of Hollywood. When Freya had first arrived in Los Angeles they had lived in one of Nicholas' enormous houses in the thick of things. Freya had hated it. Despite having lived in the hustle and bustle of London, the noise and activity of life in Hollywood had not even compared.

The house itself had been a fortress. It had been full of cameras and alarms and surrounded by an electric fence. Freya hadn't been able to live like that, so they had house-hunted.

Freya had known exactly the type of house she wanted to live in. It had been a picture she'd held in her mind from childhood when she'd been like the princess in the tower, desperate to escape. The house she saw in her mind was large and white with a big covered wooden porch outside the front door. It had a garden, with mature trees, a lawn and a swing. Inside it was modest, but most importantly it was homely. It would be somewhere she felt comfortable in and comforted by. A haven.

They had looked at a dozen houses in various towns in the vicinity of Hollywood, but as soon as they'd driven up to Whitewood House, Freya knew it was the one.

And Mayleaf, as a town, was perfect. It was small with a handful of shops and eateries, a gas station, a town hall, a high school, one bar and a diner. As clichéd as it was, it reminded Freya of every small town she'd ever seen on any American movie. But it was its sense of community Freya really loved. It was so close knit and everyone knew each other and the benefits of this far outweighed the downsides as far as she was concerned.

The town had been nothing but welcoming to Nicholas and Freya and they'd even introduced some new town laws banning journalists from entering the Town Circle. This basically meant they couldn't be pestered when they were in the town centre. It also meant they could participate in town gatherings and activities without being spied on by the press. At present the town elders were discussing whether or not to increase the boundaries of the Town Circle to incorporate Nicholas and Freya's house. That would stop the photographers congregating there.

Freya knew some of the decisions had been made because they'd made a considerable donation towards the repair of the town hall roof, but no one treated them any differently in any other respect and they both liked that.

Freya's new photography business, Exposure, had been established half an hour's drive away in the affluent city of Carlton. Freya had originally wanted to set up her business in Mayleaf itself, but there weren't suitable premises. In the end, having discussed it with Nicholas, she decided Carlton was the best option as it was closer to the main road from the airport and would be easier for people to get to.

Since her explicit photographs of Nicholas had been auctioned for charity and news of their engagement was announced, everyone who was anyone in Hollywood wanted Freya to take their picture. At first Freya found the prospect of this frightening, but having now shot dozens of A-list celebrities, it was becoming a lot more comfortable. And this morning's meeting with Sadie Fox was a chance to get into the fashion industry. That could mean big business.

If Freya was truthful she'd much rather photograph a craggy landscape or the ocean at sunset, but she knew she had a real talent for capturing something different in people when she photographed them. And she was making the most of this current popularity, taking the business, making the money and giving away the majority of it. It was her plan to benefit as many people as possible with the money. That ethic was the complete opposite to her parents and their ostentatious lifestyles. She liked being the opposite of them.

When Freya arrived at her studio her assistant, Sasha was waiting at the entrance with a polystyrene cup in one hand and a large pastry in the other.

Sasha was tall, slim, blonde and twenty five. When Freya interviewed for the position of her assistant she'd been determined to hire a man, because that was what she'd been used to. She'd also been determined not to hire anyone who was younger, slimmer or more attractive than she was, despite what employment law stipulated. However, Sasha had shown more enthusiasm in photography than the rest of the candidates put together. She was also computer literate and made good tea. There was no competition.

'Morning, Sasha, well timed as always. Mmm what flavour is this one?' Freya asked as she took the pastry and sank her teeth into it.

'It's dark chocolate today. Milo at the patisserie is trying out a new recipe and he wanted me to let him know what you think,' Sasha replied, following Freya through the reception area and into her office.

'Mmm, well tell him I love him. This is so good. Right, so, appointments for today. Sadie Fox at nine and...' Freya started, sitting down in her chair.

'Actually, Sadie Fox called earlier and she's had to cancel. She apologised and said something about having to fly to Paris urgently this morning,' Sasha informed.

'Oh no! Sasha! Why didn't you call me? I passed up sex with my fiancé for that appointment. Have you seen how attractive my fiancé is?' Freya exclaimed in horror.

'Yes I have,' Sasha said, nodding.

'You don't pass up sex with someone as handsome as that unless it's really crucial. Damn that woman!' Freya stated, leaning backwards in her chair and taking another bite of the pastry.

'I'm sorry. I didn't want to call your cell because I assumed you'd be driving,' Sasha spoke.

'Which is why they invented the hands free kit. Look, never mind. I'm sure the no sex thing can be remedied later. So, who else is booked in today?' Freya asked.

'Just someone who phoned this morning. Someone called Jonathan Sanders.'

Freya paled immediately, not certain she had heard her assistant correctly. It was a name instantly familiar to her.

'Sorry, Sasha, run that one by me again. Did you say Jonathan Sanders?' Freya checked.

'Yes I did. Is that a problem?'

'Yes. No. Well, maybe. I don't know. Was he English?' Freya asked, putting the pastry down on top of a photography magazine on her desk.

'Yes. Very well spoken.'

'Well spoken. Perhaps it isn't who I'm thinking of in that case,' Freya responded, taking a sip of her tea.

The Jonathan Sanders Freya was thinking of was the boy she'd begun dating when she was just sixteen. He'd been her first love and they'd been serious. Serious enough for Freya to tell him her real name was Jane Lawson-Peck and for her to introduce him to her parents. Days after that meeting, her father paid him to leave her and she hadn't seen him since. That was over thirteen years ago.

'Are you OK?' Sasha asked.

'Yes, yes I'm fine. What time's he coming in?" Freya asked, composing herself.

'He said he wanted to take you out to lunch, about one,' Sasha added.

'Oh, well, did he leave a number? Maybe I'll call him. I'm probably going to be tied up this lunchtime,' Freya said, using her mouse to click open her diary on the computer screen. She knew she had nothing else on but she felt uneasy about it.

'Yes he did. Here,' Sasha said and she jotted the number down on a Post-It note and passed it to Freya.

'Thanks. So, how are you doing for work today?' Freya asked her, trying to turn her attention to something other than Jonathan Sanders.

'I have an appointment. I'm having lunch with Heather Malcolm about doing some football team photos for the university. You said if she called back I could deal with it,' Sasha reminded.

'I remember. Well, if you carry on being so capable, there'll be no need for me to come here every day,' Freya remarked.

'Sorry, I just…' Sasha started.

'Sasha, I was kidding. It's fine, you're doing really well. I tell you what, tomorrow how about you and I shut ourselves in a room and go through some techniques I think will be really useful for you,' Freya suggested.

'That sounds great. I'd like that.'

'Good, well, one pastry down. What's next?' Freya asked, brushing the crumbs from her fingers.

Sasha went through the rest of the appointments for the week but Freya was unable to absorb it. The lunchtime appointment with Jonathan Sanders was disturbing her. It couldn't be the same person. It was quite a common name, and America was a big place. It was unlikely it was the same man. But Sasha said he *was* English. It could be exactly who she thought. She needed to discuss it with someone. She needed her best friend.

TWO

'Hello,' Emma's voice answered after several rings.

'Hello, Mrs P. How is that goddaughter of mine?' Freya questioned. She smiled at the sound of her best friend's voice.

'Oh hi, Freya. She's fine, asleep at the moment. I was just trying to catch up on some myself,' Emma replied.

Her friend sounded jaded.

'Oh God, I'm sorry. I didn't think. Time difference. Typical me, I'll let you go,' Freya said.

'No, no don't go. I haven't spoken to you for over a week. How is everything in the US?' Emma asked.

'The US is fine, Nick is fine, I'm fine...but Sasha's just informed me I have a lunchtime appointment with Jonathan Sanders,' Freya told her.

'Jonathan Sanders? *Your* Jonny?' Emma exclaimed.

'I don't know, but those were my first thoughts too,' Freya answered with a sigh.

'What d'you mean you don't know? You must know. I mean it's an appointment, you usually know who you're meeting. Or do they do blind appointments over there to make work more fun?' Emma questioned.

'Sasha spoke to him and made the arrangement. She said he was English but she said he was well spoken. Jonny was from Hackney. He was anything but well spoken,' Freya reminded her.

'Well, a few years have gone by. He'll be about the same age as you now. Things change, *you* can vouch for that. He might have done well for himself,' Emma suggested.

'But in what field? I mean how many fields require him to need a photographer?' Freya wanted to know.

'Perhaps he doesn't want to meet you in a business capacity. Maybe he just wants to catch up with you. I mean, you said a lunch meeting, perhaps it's just lunch.'

'But why? Why would he want lunch with me now? After all this time,' Freya questioned.

'I don't know, perhaps he saw you in a magazine or a newspaper and it brought back memories and he thought it might be nice to get in touch,' Emma suggested.

'I wonder what he's expecting me to say. I mean he dumped me, for money. That's like a red rag to a bull,' she responded, chewing a pen as she thought about it.

'Perhaps he thinks you might have calmed down about it now - because you're happy with a successful business and a wonderful man. He's probably thinking some of the angst might have evaporated,' Emma told her.

'Didn't know me very well then, did he? Angst is pretty permanent once you've pissed me off,' Freya reminded her.

'Maybe it isn't him,' Emma replied.

'Yeah you're right, it probably isn't him. It just freaked me out hearing the name,' Freya said.

'I can understand that,' Emma answered.

'But it probably isn't him,' Freya repeated.

'No,' Emma agreed.

'But what am I going to do if it's him?' Freya asked her.

'Freya! If it's him you are going to a) be professional and b) remember he's over thirty now, not the seventeen year old he was when he took the money from your father,' Emma told her.

'But I can't *not* mention that. I mean, it would be odd if I didn't, wouldn't it?'

'Why don't you see if *he* mentions it and then if you get to your desserts and he *hasn't* mentioned it, you can slip it in over coffee,' Emma suggested.

'Good idea. Now I know why I called you.'

'I'm glad no one's taken over my role even though you're living further away than ever,' Emma told her.

'You are irreplaceable. So, how's motherhood?'

'Tiring. I thought being pregnant was exhausting, but it was nothing compared to the sleep deprivation I'm suffering now,' Emma explained.

'But Yiannis is helping with the night feeding, right?' Freya checked.

'Yes, he dotes on Melly, but I'm trying to breastfeed so it's difficult to share that.'

'Urgh! God! Sorry, I know it's meant to be wonderful and natural and certainly all the A-listers are giving it a go, from what I have heard, but God, I don't think I could do it.'

'Well, it isn't easy but I'm trying to persevere.'

'I bet if it were men with the breasts, the percentage of babies being breastfed would be dramatically reduced.'

'I expect you're right.'

'Listen, I'm going to try and come and see you in the next couple of months, because I have yet to see my little godchild in the flesh,' Freya told her.

'That would be nice. How long is the flight time for you?' Emma asked.

'Don't mention the flight time or I might just hurl right now. It's something stupid like fifteen hours with a stop in Paris,' Freya said, her stomach churning at the thought of it.

'You mean Nick hasn't got a private jet.'

'Nick used to have a private jet. In fact he used to have a lot of fancy things he didn't need. I've been streamlining,' Freya answered with a smile.

'I hope Villa Kamia isn't on your "unnecessary" list just yet,' Emma said.

Villa Kamia was Nicholas' holiday home in Kassiopi, Corfu. Emma, Yiannis and Melissa were living in it while their own house was being built.

'No, don't worry. We won't be selling that any time soon. That's the one luxury item I want to hold on to,' Freya admitted.

'Well, hopefully we won't be in it for all that much longer. The builders are progressing with the house quite well.'

'Greek builders,' Freya remarked.

'Yes.'

'Greek builders progressing well,' Freya stated.

'I know what you're getting at, but it really isn't a mythical tale. They've nearly finished building the main structure. When you come over I'll take you on a tour,' Emma promised.

'I'll bring a hard hat, just in case the progress slows down between now and then.'

'You have no faith,' Emma said, laughing.

'I'm sorry. OK, well, I'd better go. It costs a fortune to phone you in the daytime. Give Melly a kiss from me and tell her Aunty Freya can't wait to cuddle her. Unsoiled of course,' Freya said.

'I will, and, Freya, give me a call later. Let me know about Jonny,' Emma ordered her.

'I will. I've decided it won't be the Jonny we know. It will be some fifty-something high roller who wants me to take some pictures of his numerous skyscrapers. I get a lot of those at the moment,' Freya said.

'Well call me anyway, but not after seven *my* time because we're trying to get Melly into a routine.'

'Noted. I'll speak to you later,' Freya ended.

As she replaced the receiver, Sasha came into the office waving a brochure in the air.

'Don't tell me! New menu for Phoenix Chinese? Gimme!' Freya said excitedly.

'No it isn't, it's the latest issue of *Entertainment Now* magazine. You and Nicholas are on the cover,' Sasha said and she put the magazine down on Freya's desk with a flourish.

'Oh, is that all? Sasha, I think we've had a conversation about this before - several conversations in fact. Having my face on the front of a magazine does nothing for me and...good God, will you look at my outfit? Someone call the fashion police. What was I thinking? Horizontal stripes do nothing for me,' Freya announced, as she picked up the magazine and studied it more closely.

'I think it's quite a nice picture. See how the photographer got the light just right? I think this was taken around dusk, going by the shadows,' Sasha told her.

'Are you trying to impress me, Sasha? This picture was taken when we visited the Carlton General

Hospital to donate some money. It was definitely dusky, good spot,' Freya answered her.

'Whoever took it has captured Nick really well,' Sasha said, studying the photograph.

'He's the most photogenic person I know. I could take a picture of him sat on the toilet and he would still come out looking amazing. Note the hint of jealousy.'

'He has a great bone structure.'

'Yes he does. But enough now or next you'll be asking for a poster to go above your bed,' Freya said.

She picked up the magazine and dropped it in the bin.

'Sorry,' Sasha apologised.

'That's OK. It's you and half of the female population of the world. I am one lucky lady, but don't worry, I *do* know it,' Freya answered with a smile.

As she had no appointments that morning, Freya took her equipment and drove to County Bridge. County Bridge was ten miles north of Carlton and one of the five old bridges, all in a thirty mile radius of the city. Freya had been told about their existence by Casey, who ran the diner in Mayleaf. Their history was they were over a hundred years old and had been built by a group of Christians for the purpose of giving the surrounding towns easy access across the river to the area's churches. All of the bridges were different in their style. Two had arches, two had a straight design and County Bridge, Freya's particular favourite, was a mixture of both. That bridge had an inscription on one of the spindles halfway across which read *Glory to the Father, leave sorrow behind and take hope from the past.*

Freya had taken to photographing all the bridges and had built up quite a collection of pictures. Her favourite time of day for capturing them was in the early morning when the mist was on the water and the sun was just starting to rise. It was important to have the light just right when taking photos of the bridges, as unlike most of the wooden structures in the area, the Christian Fathers Bridges, as they were known, were painted black.

Freya stood on one side of the river and waited for the bird she was watching to land on the bridge. It was a black crow with a huge beak, scanning the water for flies it was chasing and catching. It flapped its wings and Freya took a picture.

Crows were the only birds she had ever seen at the bridges. It surprised her as the surrounding area was grass and marsh. She would have expected to see a more varied selection of birds. She'd also never seen any fish in the river near the bridges, although she knew further downstream there was an abundance of trout and carp. She knew this because whenever she walked along the bank to take photographs of the bridges up stream, there were usually at least two or three fishermen.

The crow left the bridge and Freya took her favourite camera, Claude, away from her eye and let it hang from her neck. She named all her cameras and Claude was given to her by Nicholas as a late birthday present just after they first met.

Freya walked across the bridge and stopped in the middle to read the inscription as she did every time she visited.

'Glory to the Father, leave sorrow behind and take hope from the past,' Freya spoke out loud.

She ran her fingers across the words, feeling the indents made in the black wood. Freya had interpreted it to mean there had been sorrow in the present for the Christian Fathers and they were taking hope from the past when their religion was founded. But perhaps she was wrong.

A crow let out a loud squawk and Freya flinched, the noise interrupting, the stillness startling her. She looked at her watch and saw it was almost quarter to one. Jonathan Sanders would be arriving at the office in just over fifteen minutes. If she didn't hurry she'd be late and she really wanted to be in her office and composed before he arrived, just in case. She had chickened out of calling him. She was certain it wouldn't be Jonny from London. Why would it be? They had no unfinished business as far as she was concerned.

She hurried across the bridge and headed back to her SUV, leaving County Bridge, silent and deserted.

Three

By the time she arrived back at the office Freya was red in the face and sweating. There had been awful traffic on the main road and she'd had an altercation with a teenage driver of a Carlton Cookies van who pulled out in front of her from a side street. If she didn't love those cookies so much she would've given the driver a piece of her mind. She could have haggled for a large box of white chocolate chip.

She locked the car and jogged towards the office, Claude still swinging from her neck. She hesitated before she went to push open the door. She could see through the glass. If she did step inside she'd come face-to-face with Jonathan Sanders. The Jonathan Sanders she hadn't seen since she was seventeen. It was him.

He was sat in one of the leather chairs in the reception area and Avril, the part time receptionist, was pouring him some coffee. Freya swallowed as she looked at him. He was wearing an expensive dark suit, with a white shirt and a dark grey tie. He looked smart and business-like. His hair was still jet black. His eyes that chocolately dark brown. But now he had a short beard, no more than stubble really. It suited him.

He looked up from the cup of coffee and glanced over at the door. Freya pushed quickly and fixed a smile on her face. She needed to remain in control of this meeting.

'Jonny,' she greeted hurriedly. She moved towards him, hand outstretched.

He stood up, put the coffee cup on the small table next to him and took hold of her hand.

'Hello, Freya,' he greeted, shaking her hand.

And then, before she could do anything about it, he drew her towards him and kissed her first on one cheek and then the other.

'Well, someone has been brushing up on their greeting etiquette, haven't they?' Freya remarked awkwardly, knowing her cheeks were flushing.

'You look great,' he told her. He looked her up and down.

'You always did know how to compliment a girl,' she replied. She was moving from one foot to the other, unable to stand still. Awkward.

'I thought we could go out for lunch, if you don't have any other plans,' Jonathan suggested.

'Well, I...' Freya started. She looked across at Avril who was now sat back behind the reception desk.

'There are some messages, but nothing looks urgent,' Avril announced.

'Well that's good. Then we can go. Yes?" Jonathan asked Freya.

'I guess so. I'll just ditch Claude,' Freya said, pulling the camera up from around her neck.

'The camera? Oh no, don't leave that behind. I've got something I would like you to see,' he said.

'That sounds intriguing. Before or after lunch?'

'After, I think. I remember you can't usually make it past one without needing something to eat,' Jonathan said, smiling. The smile was still as charming.

'Things do change you know," Freya stated. She was angry but she didn't really know why. Having him here was upsetting her new balance. He was part of her past. The past she'd tried hard to put behind her.

'I know they do, but are you telling me your stomach isn't crying out for a pizza right now?' Jonathan asked her.

She could almost taste it the second the words were out of his mouth.

'We're going for pizza? Well, why didn't you say? Lead on,' she responded. She took a breath, replaced her smile and waved an arm at the door.

They left the office and Jonathan led the way towards a sleek, grey Chrysler 300c SRT8 parked in the car park.

'This is never your car,' she exclaimed, snorting with laughter.

'What's so amusing? You don't like it?' he asked her. He opened the back door for her.

'No, it's fine. It's very posh. I just never saw you as a business executive. And believe me, this car has "business executive" written all over it,' Freya said. She ran her hand along the boot. This car was worth a fortune. It was either an extravagant purchase or Jonny was working for someone like Donald Trump.

'What did you think I would end up being, Freya?' he asked. He met her eyes with his.

'I don't know. When you left me I guess I hoped you would end up being a bin man or something,' Freya admitted. That sounded bitter but at least she'd been honest.

'Well, I'm sorry to disappoint you, but I did a little better than that. So, are you going to get in?' he asked, indicating the open door.

'In the back? Are we really going to relive old times? Because looking in there I have to say it isn't a patch on the Ford Cortina,' Freya joked. That had come out dry and embarrassing but she didn't know what else to say. She didn't know why he was here.

'I have a driver,' he said.

'What?! You have a driver! Now you *are* kidding me,' Freya exclaimed. She poked her head into the car. Looking up into the driver's seat she saw the driver. Peaked cap, blue uniform, sat ready to set off.

'I'm sorry but this is unreal. When we last saw each other you lived on a council estate, you weren't doing so well at college and you rode around on a BMX,' Freya reminded him.

'As you said, things change. Now, are we going for lunch so I can tell you what else has changed or do you want to stand in the car park all day being photographed by those journalists over there?' Jonathan asked. He jerked his thumb behind him. Two men with cameras were hovering around by the gateway to the building.

'I'll be wanting a stuffed crust and garlic bread to start,' Freya told him. She also needed olives and pudding was a must, but that could wait until the restaurant. The stuffed crust was the deal breaker.

'I'm sure that can be arranged.'

The car drove them into the centre of Carlton and stopped outside La Luna, the most expensive Italian restaurant in the city. Freya and Nicholas had been there once and the food was excellent, but the prices were astronomical.

'Money is obviously no object to you then,' Freya said as they entered the restaurant.

'No it isn't. Does that bother you? Because I would have thought, having a rich boyfriend, you would have become reacquainted with wealth.' One of the restaurant staff took his jacket from him.

'Wealth and I have a rather complicated relationship as you know. It seems I have it whether I want it or not and it does act a little dejected when I try and give it all away.'

'I haven't forgotten you cut up your mother's store cards. I shall be keeping my American Express close to my chest,' Jonathan assured her.

'If it's really that important to you, you can get it its own chair and napkin.'

'Your usual table, Mr Sanders?'

The manager of the restaurant greeted them in the lobby.

'Please and could you arrange a bottle of your best cabernet sauvignon,' Jonathan ordered.

'Certainly, Sir. Good afternoon, Miss Johnson, how are you?' the manager asked, turning to Freya.

'I'm fine thanks, Frank. Can I have olives? You know, the Greek ones?'

'Of course. Please, come this way.' He led them into the dining room.

'Your "usual" table?' Freya remarked as she walked alongside Jonathan towards a table at the back of the room.

'Yes, I come to Carlton every three or four months. I try to eat here as often as I can when I'm in town. They do fantastic pasta.'

'You eat pasta! I have to tell you, Jonny I'm finding this transformation of yours a little difficult to take in. The smart clothes. The business man's car. The change in diet. The goatee. Next you'll be telling me you have a mansion in Beverley Hills,' Freya said.

'Just off of Santa Monica Boulevard actually.'

Four

'You live in America?' Freya questioned.

She put the menu down and stared across at him. Ordering food could wait. She wanted to hear his story.

'Some of the time. I travel,' he answered. He poured some bottled water into Freya's glass.

'So, what's your business? What do you do?'

'Business*es*. My main occupation – I'm a developer. I see things with potential and I try to bring that out,' he stated.

'Please tell me you aren't one of those people who evicts, demolishes and builds office towers,' Freya begged. She couldn't think of anything worse. Well, perhaps someone who was paid to bang on about eating five-a-day.

'I try not to do that too often. But sometimes it's unavoidable.'

'Oh my God, you are. Well now I know why you have bullet-proof glass on that car.'

'I head up corporations, Freya. Corporations with shareholders that want returns for their investment. They're my priority and, like I said, building office towers on residential areas really isn't my bag. Hotels and inns are more my specialty. Have you heard of the Recuperation Inns?' he asked.

'Yes of course, they have billboards everywhere with a really cheesy slogan. Something like *the ultimate sleep sensation begins at a Recuperation*. If that's your company I would shoot your ad man,' she replied.

'But you remembered it, so he's done his job. That is one of my companies and it's my aim to have a Recuperation Inn in every major city in the US by the time I retire. I'm hopeful for forty, so I've got just under ten years,' he said. He smiled. It looked smug-arsed.

'My, my, what happened? Did you enter *The Apprentice* or something? If I remember right, you were studying mechanics at college,' Freya said.

'I can still change a tyre but I also learnt how to run a multi-million pound organisation.'

'Well good for you. I hope you and your hotels will be very happy together. I'll have garlic bread, a pizza with everything on it and tell them not to hold back on those olives,' Freya told him. She pushed the menu away.

'Fine and how about some banoffee pie for dessert?' he suggested.

'Whatever.'

She was cross. Why was she cross? Why didn't she want him to be successful? Because he had left her and humiliated her and taken money from her father. But that was years ago and she had a great life now and a wonderful partner to share it with. Why did she want to think of Jonny back on that council estate amounting to nothing? When had she got so cruel?

Frank returned with the wine and Jonathan gave their order.

'You're still angry with me, aren't you?' Jonathan said after Frank left.

'And why would I be angry with you, Jonny?'

'Freya, I have to say it makes me feel seventeen again, you calling me that. No one calls me that anymore,' he admitted. He laughed, then smiled, the brown eyes crinkling at the edges.

'Well, what would you rather I call you? Money-grabbing weasel? Two-faced hypocrite?'

Her temper rose in her gut, her face flamed. She stared him down.

'I'm not either of those things,' he insisted. He took a sip of his wine. He looked cool and collected, unfazed by her name-calling.

'No? Well, what would you call someone who did what you did to me? If there's another name for it then hit me with it.'

'You don't know the full story.'

'Yes I do. Emma told me what happened. My father paid you off. He gave you money to stop seeing me and you took it,' Freya stated through gritted teeth.

It still stung. The memories burned.

'That isn't strictly true.'

'No? Well, what did I leave out? One minute you were telling me you didn't care who I really was, or who my father was. You said you wanted to marry me. The next minute you won't answer my calls or see me. Then Emma is telling me you're leaving the area,' Freya continued.

'It wasn't because I didn't love you anymore. It was just complicated.'

'You mean *I* was complicated. *I* was suddenly too complicated for you to deal with. So, it had nothing to do with thirty thousand pounds?' Freya asked.

How was he going to squirm out of that one?

'No. It had nothing to do with thirty thousand pounds.'

'Well, what was it then? Fifty? A hundred thousand? My father is a very rich man, perhaps it was more than that. A million? No, I don't think he would part with that much just to stop me seeing someone he didn't approve of,' Freya carried on.

She was aware her voice had almost hit banshee heights and a table to their left was now paying more attention to them than the food. She didn't care. She wanted to get this out. She needed him to know how much he had hurt her and find out why.

'Eric didn't give me any money,' Jonathan told her.

She closed her lips, narrowed her eyes and waited for him to say something else. There had to be something else. He took another sip of his wine, his gaze not leaving hers.

If her father hadn't given him money to leave her, then why had he left her? And why had Emma told her that Jonathan had accepted money from her father to not see her again.

'I don't understand. So, you just left because he told you to? You gave up what we had together because my father asked you to?' she stuttered.

'I left because my father got a new job on the other side of London. It was a good job, it paid well and it was a step up for us,' he explained.

'I don't believe you. You don't break up with someone just because you're moving a few miles away. The whole of London is connected by something called The Tube for God's sake. We could have met up, we could have carried on.'

She didn't believe this. All this time she had thought everything had come down to money again and he was here telling her something different. What did she believe?

'I didn't want to carry on, like I said, it was too complicated.' There was strength to his tone, finality.

'Hang on a minute here. I'm old enough to be able to take the truth that maybe you didn't want to date me anymore, although I find that a little difficult to believe, seeing as you'd got down on your knee and proposed to me, albeit with a ring from Argos. But why tell Emma my father paid you off?'

'I don't know. Because I was seventeen and immature and I knew you would believe it. I was scared, Freya. Meeting your parents and actually thinking properly about making a commitment and settling down, it freaked me out. I wasn't really ready,' he admitted. He let out an audible sigh.

'So, rather than tell me that, you made up a story about my father paying you to leave and you had me believe that story for all this time? Wait a minute, this doesn't add up. I've told my father on more than one occasion that I blamed him for making you leave and he's never contradicted me. Why would he take the blame if he wasn't involved?'

Her brain was working overtime now. None of this made sense and she was struggling to fit the pieces together.

'I don't know. I can't comment on anything Eric might or might not have said. But I'm telling you now, he did not pay me to leave you. It was my decision, I made it on my own and I apologise if I upset you.'

'Upset me? I wouldn't say the house burning was entirely down to you leaving me, but it was a contributing factor. My God, all this time I've been thinking it was my evil father at work again and it was just a normal dumping scenario.'

She'd been jilted, plain and simple. That thought had her reaching for her wineglass and pouring it into the mouth.

'Like I said, it was complicated,' Jonathan repeated.

'Sure, whatever.'

She felt sick.

'Look, surely we can move on from this. I mean we were both young and immature and these things happen. And you're engaged now. Tell me about Nicholas Kaden,' he urged.

'Nick's the most amazing man I've ever met. He's kind of a male version of me, without the temper and obviously slimmer. But he does have a soft spot for takeaways and I'm teaching him that leftovers really are nice on toast for breakfast.'

'He's developing your discerning palate then,' Jonathan remarked, a smile on his lips.

'He's trying.' She smiled as she thought about her fiancé. 'He's just really special and unlike some of the men I've dated, he's realised the importance and unimportance of money.'

'I can understand why that'd be vital to you.'

'God, Jonny, I'm so mad at you right now. I don't know whether I can sit here and be adult about this,' she admitted, blowing out a breath.

'I'd like it if you did. If only for the food. Besides, I do have a proposition for you. This *is* a business lunch,' he told her.

'Why do I get the feeling this is going to be something I'm likely to oppose?'

'I'm not going to bulldoze Mayleaf if that's what you're thinking. Besides, the town elders are pretty scary characters. I wouldn't like to cross those guys.'

'Then what *are* you going to do? Build a Recuperation Inn on top of Exposure?' she asked.

'Let's eat, then I'll show you.'

Five

'You enjoyed the food?' Jonathan asked. They were in back in the Chrysler heading off in an easterly direction.

'Yes, it was good. I enjoyed it all the more because you were paying,' she admitted.

She would pay later because she could barely move with the amount she'd stuffed in. If the car went any quicker she was likely to lose it all over the leather upholstery.

'You must be a breath of fresh air to the world of celebrity, Freya. Tell me, do you still raid the discounted items at the grocery stores?'

'Sometimes, but more often than not I buy double what I need and drop into a soup kitchen on the way home. And I don't do that for the publicity, I do that because I can. And I have to tell you, it gives me more satisfaction to see an old man with holes in his clothes and nothing on his feet eating a good meal in a warm place, than it does to eat an expensive Italian meal.'

'I heard you talk on Atlantic FM about the homeless. I found it very moving,' Jonathan admitted.

'The homeless are a project of mine at the moment. I'm in the process of setting up a centre to provide accommodation and food. It sort of started out as a vision for a hostel and then it turned into something bigger than that. I want somewhere that provides counselling and advice, skills to get people jobs and support for when they can leave the centre and get a place of their own.'

She felt more passionately about the homeless shelter project than she did about anything else in her life. There was something about giving people with nothing help to start over again that struck a chord with her.

'It sounds like it's something close to your heart.'

'Nick took me to where he used to live when he was struggling to raise his brother. The number of homeless people there is well above the national average and these people are of all ages and backgrounds and some are children. I was appalled and I said we had to do something about it. So, to start with I bought out the stock in two clothes stores and we handed it all out. Then we decided, to make a real difference, it would take more than just a handout. That's when I decided to set up the Every Day project,' she explained.

'I know.'

'What? What d'you mean you know?'

The Every Day project was new, very new. Only their closest advisors knew of their plans. Nothing had even been drafted for the release to the press yet.

'I know about your charity, the Every Day project. I made a bid for the same piece of land your first centre is going to be built on,' he told her.

'That was all done anonymously and no one knew what that was for. How?'

'I know a lot of people.'

'So, what happened? You couldn't outbid me? That I don't believe.'

She was angry again. What was it with this man? Why was he back poking his nose into her life? What did he want? There had to be something.

'Oh, I could have outbid you but I took the time and trouble to investigate that fake name you used. I wanted to find out who I was really up against. When I found out I decided you were too formidable a force.' He smiled.

'Conscience get the better of you?'

'Something like that. I admire your selflessness, Freya. I really do.' There was sincerity in his expression.

'Don't admire me. There isn't anything special about what I'm doing. I'm just making the most of what I have by spreading it around a bit,' she told him.

'Do you not think you could have done that if you'd stayed with your family? Taken your trust fund at eighteen and given it to Save the Whale or something?'

'My father would never have given me anything unless I changed how I felt about his world. I couldn't do that, not even for pretence. I'm a black and white person, Jonny, you know that. There are no grey areas with me.' She pulled her head up to meet his eyes and jutted her chin out. She hoped it spelt out her determination.

'I guess not. Well, here we are,' he announced as the car came to a halt at the edge of a minor road.

He got out and walked around to open her door.

'Here we are? We're in Gatebrook, near Covenant Bridge. There's nothing here but the river, the bridge and the old church. No one lives here,' Freya said. She stepped out of the car, the biting wind chilling her to the bone. She wished she'd brought a jacket.

'No one lives here at the moment. But they could do, in a year or so,' he said. He walked off the road and onto the grassland.

'I'm not with you.'

'This land belongs to me,' he announced. He spread his arms wide and let out a satisfied laugh.

'You bought the field? Isn't it a little out of the way for a Recuperation Inn? The nearest petrol station is at least three miles away,' Freya commented.

'I bought the town of Gatebrook, from boundary to boundary. Isn't it great? I own the church, the bridge and all this grass.' He was really going for it with the laughter now. It was like JR Ewing nailing an important oil deal.

'You own one of the Christian Fathers bridges? But they're protected, aren't they?'

The thought of him taking a wrecking ball to one of her much loved sites would be the final nail in their relationship. She might even have to vomit up the lunch if that's what he was telling her.

'Everyone has a price, Freya,' he answered.

'God, now you're starting to sound like my father.'

'So, what do you think?" He turned to her, loosened his tie a little. He looked like he was waiting for her to answer favourably.

'I think if you're considering building one of those hotel monstrosities on this land then you're going to have a lot of local opposition. In fact *I* will start the protest.'

She'd heard enough and her stomach was protesting. She began to walk back to the car.

'And what if I was going to create a purpose-built village with houses for the homeless, shops and businesses to create jobs for them and a school for their children?' he called.

That got her attention. She turned back around to face him. She saw his expression was serious, not a hint of humour on his face.

'I think your cause is really something the government should be providing. But, seeing as there's a void there, I think your charity is exactly what's needed. I like the idea of satisfying a need and providing opportunities. It's caring coupled with self-improvement and I think it will work,' he finished.

'Be careful, Jonny. Your mask of ruthlessness is slipping.'

'This isn't business. This is giving something back. Giving something back to you,' he stated.

'You don't owe me anything. I kept the Argos ring. It's mounted,' she replied quickly.

'I'm serious, Freya. I really want to do this and I *am* doing this, whether you want me to or not.'

'What's the catch? There has to be one.'

'No catch.'

'No catch?' Freya queried.

'Well, I would like you to take some photographs for the Recuperation Inns, but it isn't a deal breaker. Whatever you say to that, I'll still go ahead with the Every Day project,' he assured her.

She looked at him. Jonny Sanders. Who was this man stood before her? He'd let her down before. Could she trust him with a project that meant so much?

'Freya, I mean what I say. No hidden agendas,' he reiterated.

She nodded.

'Well then, I think it's an amazing idea. I mean, here would be a perfect location and…'

'Can we be friends?' he interrupted.

'Look, this is all very weird, Jonny. It's been so many years and I've tried so hard to put that life behind me, I don't…' she started.

'It would mean a lot to me, Freya. I know what I did was wrong and I can only put it down to being a stupid teenage… "dirt bag" I think is the term over here,' he spoke.

He looked sorry. He looked genuine. What he was offering was more than she dared to believe.

'How much is all this going to cost your company?' she asked.

'I have no idea and…who cares?' He smiled and shrugged his shoulders.

'Come here then, friend. Have a hug.' She opened her arms to him.

He put his arms around her and held her tightly against him.

'This hug feels good,' he admitted.

'Yes it does.'

It also felt truly awkward and was bringing back so many memories of the past. She let him go and stepped away, straightening her top. She hugged her arms around herself trying to stave off the winter wind.

'Well, let's head back to Exposure and we can make an appointment for you to start photographing the Recuperations,' he suggested.

'I haven't agreed to that yet. And as far as I can remember, most of the buildings are really ugly,' Freya said, screwing up her face.

'Cost was taken into account when they were designed but we do offer you a choice from ten different textures of pillows,' Jonathan reminded her.

'And five different coloured bath robes,' Freya added.

'You really have stayed in one.'

'We were very desperate at the time, but I do still have the red bathrobe.'

'The red ones are in short supply. A popular colour with the clients that want to take a souvenir home with them,' he teased.

'What are you insinuating?'
'Absolutely nothing. I wouldn't dare.'

Six

When Freya arrived home that evening Nicholas was sat in the garden, his back to the house, reading through a script. Freya crept out of the patio doors and walked on tiptoes towards him, hoping to catch him by surprise. It was only when she was caught by a gust of icy wind she saw he was wearing a sweater and perhaps she should have thought about a coat.

'You would never make it as an assassin,' he said as Freya stopped just behind his chair.

'Oh, how did you know I was there?' Freya asked, disappointed.

'Did you not see Willis climb out of the tree licking his mouth at the prospect of Mommy arriving home to feed him treats? Here he comes now. Hey, boy, you ruined Mommy's surprise.' Willis nuzzled his hand and then weaved in and out of Freya's legs.

'I told you he was clever and it's *Mummy*! He isn't bilingual you know. He recognises English not American. Anyway, have you had a good day? You're tired aren't you? Hallmark channel a bit emotionally draining?' Freya asked, kissing him on the lips then sitting in the chair opposite him.

She could have done with a blanket.

'Yeah I'm tired. How did you know? Not looking so hot?' he asked.

'You're wearing your glasses. You always wear your glasses when you're tired.'

'My God, you know all this and we aren't even married yet.'

'So, how did your meeting with the writer guy go?' Freya asked.

'It was fine. We've done my childhood now and looking after Matt, so we're just about to get into the realms of the Cheesy Twangers commercial and my first movie role, freaky hairstyle and all.'

'Oh, I was hoping you would have skipped to the chapter about meeting me. After all, that's when your life really began.'

'I've told him that already. I said *Mark, we can get through all this real quick because my life meant nothing until I met my fiancée.* He said we had to go through the motions. But trust me, your chapter is the centre of the story. The rest is just padding,' he assured her.

'You're good.'

'Hey, never mind my book. How did it go with Sadie Fox? You didn't call me. I said give me a call and let me know how it went.' He took off his glasses and rubbed at his eyes.

'I didn't call because there was nothing to report. She cancelled me. Gave Sasha some excuse about having to fly to Paris. I think it's more likely she's found another photographer,' Freya told him.

'Well, that's her loss. I wouldn't lose any sleep over it.'

'No, I know, I won't. So, did you pick up the fancy dress outfits for tonight?'

'Yes I did.'

'And have you looked at them yet?' She grinned.

'Yes I have.'

'And what do you think?'

'Please tell me I'm the doctor and not the nurse.'

She let out a scream of laughter and rocked back and forth in her chair. Willis darted for the safety of the house.

'No, Freya! No way! I am not dressing up in a nurse's outfit! Absolutely not!' he exclaimed.

'But Nick, the doctor's outfit was the only one they had in my size, apart from the Darth Vader costume. And I just couldn't visualise how I was going to eat with the mask on or talk without scaring Sam and Jolie's kids,' she explained.

All lies. She'd seen the nurse costume and thought it would be perfect for him.

'I'm not doing it, Freya. I mean it.'

'Come on, you *so* have the legs for it,' she cajoled.

'There's nothing you can say to persuade me into that outfit. Nothing,' he insisted. He picked up his glass of orange juice and drank it down.

'Oh no? Are you sure about that?' She ran her hand slowly up the inside of his thigh.

'Have you seen the length of the skirt? It's practically obscene,' he continued.

'You. Me. A bottle of wine and candles. Some soft music, maybe Luther Vandross or Lionel Richie. A plate of soft fruits and double cream. We could light the fire and close the blinds and…' Freya began. She slipped her hand up inside his t-shirt and caressed his stomach with her fingers.

'I'm not wearing high shoes with it. Or stockings,' he answered.

'I'll go and open the wine, you grab Luther.'

Sam and Jolie's home was inside the Town Circle and only a few minutes walk from Whitewood House. The party had been due to start at seven but at seven forty Nicholas still wasn't ready.

'What are you doing in there, Nick? We're going to be late,' Freya called to him.

She stood outside the bathroom door, dressed in a blue surgeon's outfit complete with head scarf.

'I don't know whether I can actually allow *you* to see this, let alone half the town,' he called back.

'Get out here, Matron. My blood pressure is rising,' she teased, laughing.

'Just give me another five. I'm coming to terms with it.'

'OK...oh that's the phone now. If it's for you I'll tell them you're just slipping your petticoat on.'

'You will not! Freya!' Nicholas shouted.

She went into their bedroom and picked up the phone from the nightstand.

'Hello.'

'Hello, this is Mrs P calling,' Emma's voice said.

'Em, what time is it over there? I was going to ring but I didn't want to wake up Melly.'

'You don't want to know what time it is but I'm awake, just. I thought I'd ring and find out what happened today. Was it Jonny?'

'Hang on.' She stood up and closed the bedroom door.

'Freya?'

'I'm here, but so is Nick. I haven't told him about Jonny yet,' she whispered.

'You mean it *was* him. My God,' Emma stated.

'Yes it was him and Em, you should see him. You would hardly recognise him. He's been completely swallowed up by commerce and industry,' Freya told her.

'He's in business? What sort of business? What did he look like? Last time I saw him he was really skinny and had shoulder-length hair.'

'Still skinny but very different hair. Have you heard of the Recuperation Inns? They're a big chain of hotels over here.'

'No, but go on.'

'Well Jonny owns them. Them and countless other investments from what I can make out. He's practically as wealthy as my father,' Freya informed her.

'I don't believe it! Jonny Sanders the millionaire?! That is just so hard to imagine.'

'I barely recognised him. He has a goatee and his hair is short and he was wearing a Versace suit. Versace!'

'And what did he want? Did he just want to catch up or did he want you to take some photographs?'

'Well yes he did want my services, but there was more to it than that. He's bought a huge plot of land about twenty miles from here. He says he's going to develop it into a village for my Every Day project. It's going to be a proper community where people can be given a fresh start in life with training and tuition. There'd be jobs and a school,' she started to explain.

'That sounds fantastic but what would make him want to do that? And how did he know about your charity? I thought it was all still under wraps.'

'He made a bid for the site at Chesterville. Then he dug around.'

'And did you discuss what happened before? About him taking the money from your father?'

'Yes, funnily enough it did come up. He claims my father had nothing to do with it. He says it was all too much for him, the commitment, meeting my parents and realising just what that entailed. He said it was his decision and he chickened out of telling me the truth, so he made up the story about my father paying him off.'

The tale she was recounting sounded as believable as an *X-Files* script. But he'd told her and she'd believed him. Hadn't she? Or had her opinion been blighted by the promise of help for the Every Day project?

'So he lied to me! Did you believe him?'

Did she?

'I don't know. It was strange, seeing him again and him being so different to how I remember.'

Had she been charmed by the good stuff from the past? The chocolate brown eyes, the friendly hug at Gatebrook?

'So, will you see him again do you think?'

'Well, he's going to be donating a lot of money to my charity, and I mean *a lot* of money. Millions of dollars. In return I said I'd do some promotional pictures for the Recuperation Inns. Vulgar buildings though they are,' Freya told her.

'I can't believe he's rich. I just can't imagine it. I mean one of the reasons you dated him in the first place was because he was just the opposite of what you were,' Emma reminded.

'I know and now he's practically Trumpesque. It's a rags to riches tale if ever there was one. Perhaps there's a film in it,' Freya joked.

'So, why haven't you told Nick about meeting with him?'

Good question, best friend. Why hadn't she told Nick about meeting Jonny? *Think of an answer, anything will do.*

'Oh, I don't know. It was weird, you know, and it hasn't sunk in properly yet. I just want to get it straight in my head first before I tell Nick.'

'And that's all it is? There were no old feelings being stirred up when you saw him? I mean, you did want to marry him once.'

'Yeah, I know, but it was a long time ago,' Freya reminded her.

'And he *was* the only man before Nick that you admitted your identity to,' Emma continued.

'There were no old feelings being stirred up. Apart from this amazing thing he's doing for my charity, he's driven by profit and that makes him very unattractive. Actually he gave me a hug when we were out at Gatebrook and it felt just plain weird,' Freya said, remembering the moment.

'How d'you mean?'

'I don't know. It was odd. It felt awkward and just off. Anyway, it didn't make me feel anything remotely like *God, my first love, how I want him back*,' Freya concluded.

'Then I'd tell Nick you met with him and what he's going to do for the charity in case he jumps to the wrong conclusion. You know what men are like about things being kept from them, particularly with regard to exes.'

'Yes, I do remember quiet, mild-mannered Yiannis fighting with Dopey Darren in the fountain.'

'Exactly, so what time is it there? What am I interrupting?'

'It's nearly eight at night and we're going to a friend's birthday party. Sam. Him and Jolie run the local store,' Freya told her.

'The couple with twin boys you call Krueger One and Krueger Two,' Emma said.

'Yes, that's them. It's fancy dress and Nick's holed up in the bathroom because he's a little uncomfortable with his outfit.' She laughed.

'What have you got him dressed in?'

'A nurse costume!'

Emma let out a shriek and both the women split their sides with laughter.

Seven

'You can see my ass in this uniform,' Nicholas said, pulling at the hem of the skirt.

'Can you? Let me look.'

He'd insisted they called a cab so he didn't have the humiliation of walking past the photographers at their front gate. Now they were outside Sam and Jolie's home in the centre of Mayleaf.

'I'm freezing,' he complained as they waited on the doorstep for someone to arrive.

'I did say you should wear tights but Mr Macho wasn't having any of it, was he? If you go down with the flu don't blame me. Are we expecting snow? I thought snow didn't exist in Hollywood,' Freya said, pulling her surgical rubber gloves further up her arm.

'I don't believe they didn't have a nurse costume in your size.'

'Nick, you know if you're bigger than Barbie here you don't count. It's just a knock on effect. You should campaign,' Freya told him.

'Nick! Freya! You made it! My God, Nick, you're certainly making a statement with that costume,' Jolie announced, opening the door. She was dressed in a cowgirl outfit.

'Is it OK if I carry on with the statement making in front of your fire?' he asked, stepping past Freya.

'Sure, come on in guys,' Jolie invited, making way for them to enter.

Jolie was thirty five and a mother of two six year old boys, Michael and Adrian. She and her husband, Sam, ran Mayleaf's convenience store and were an integral part of town life. Jolie took the minutes of the town meetings and Sam was a member of the Town Festival committee.

'Jolie, I'm sorry we're late. I got talking on the phone and Nick was having a prima donna moment over his outfit,' Freya said, entering the house.

'That's OK, you've only missed Brian trying to rescue the boys' football from the tree and falling head first into the compost.'

'Oh you're kidding me? I missed the "Brian Episode"! How could that happen so early on in the evening? Nick, I missed the "Brian Episode",' Freya announced, disappointed.

'I have no doubt it won't be the only one of the evening. Hey, where's the birthday guy?' Nicholas asked Jolie.

'Straight through, into the den. He's set up a bar in there. We were thinking of going out in the garden but boy it's gotten cold.'

'Drink, Freya?' Nicholas asked her.

'Yes please.' She followed Jolie into the kitchen.

'I'm so glad you two could come tonight. I know how busy you both are,' Jolie said, picking up some napkins and glasses.

'We wouldn't have missed it for the world. You and Sam have been so great to us since we moved here,' Freya said, taking some of the glasses from Jolie.

'Come through and have some food,' Jolie said. She led the way into the large family room at the back of the house.

'Hey, Freya, I like your costume and as for Nick's, well, I've suggested to him he ought to think about taking on a different role in his next movie. Maybe a sequel to *Tootsie*. What do you think?' Sam called. The store owner was dressed as Dracula.

'Now do you see what you've done, babe? I'm the town clown,' Nicholas said. He straightened his face and then broke it with a laugh.

'If only your millions of adoring fans could see you now,' Freya said, taking the beer Nicholas was offering her.

'I think you look great, Nick. Take no notice of the old man,' Jolie said, smiling.

'Ha! She's been calling me "the old man" since I got up this morning. You would think I'd turned fifty not forty.'

'Well, I don't think you look a day over thirty nine and this is a little gift from us. Happy birthday,' Freya said. She passed Sam a gift-wrapped box and kissed him on the cheek.

'Oh thanks, guys. You didn't have to get me anything,' Sam said.

'What is it, Dad? What is it? Get off me, Adrian. I want to see!' Michael (Krueger One) shouted, pushing his brother out of the way in order to watch his father open up the present.

'The boys bought him a remote control jeep, which of course they both wanted to play with. Sam liked it so much they haven't had a chance to have a go yet,' Jolie told Freya.

Sam unwrapped the present, opened the box and revealed a watch.

'Whoa! Is that real gold?!' Adrian (Krueger Two) shouted out loudly. He tried to grab the box from his father.

'Nick, Freya, this is too much. I don't know what to say,' Sam spoke, running his fingers over the watch and admiring it.

'Don't say anything. It's your fortieth birthday. You have to have some nice treats on your fortieth birthday. Besides, it isn't real gold. But don't tell the boys,' Freya whispered, smiling.

'It's great, thank you both. Here Jolie, take a look," Sam said, passing the box over to his wife.

Nicholas took Freya by the arm and gently pulled her towards him.

'I thought you didn't believe in extravagance,' he whispered to her.

'I don't know what you mean.' She took a swig of her beer.

'You bought Sam a gold watch.'

'No flies on you is there.'

'I had one just like it until you made me auction it off,' Nicholas replied.

'I wanted to get Sam something nice and I never said we couldn't splash out on our friends. It's just *unnecessary* extravagance that pisses me off, like you having *five* different expensive watches and only two arms to wear them on. Or the fact you used to have *four* cars and only ever drove one of them.'

'Alright, you've made your point.'

'He will treasure that watch and now he thinks it isn't real he'll wear it every day at the store. That will give me a little rush of pleasure every time I see it on his wrist,' Freya explained.

'If he doesn't get mugged for it.'

'You're a killjoy, Nursie and I cannot take you seriously while you're wearing a dress.'

'Well, Doctor, if you promise me a large dose of your bedside manner later I might let you take it off,' Nicholas whispered to her.

'Hello, Freya, would you like a cup cake? I made them myself,' Brian announced. He appeared at her side, holding a tray of cakes coated in pink icing.

'Oh did you? Well, Brian, I will take one for later because I think Sam's starting the barbecue. I hope we're staying indoors to eat. Are we expecting snow?' Freya asked, taking a cake.

'Just to let you know, I ran out of sugar halfway through the recipe so I used bicarbonate of soda instead. Adrian says they taste different to the ones his mother makes,' Brian told her.

'I suspect they do. Are you noting this? "Brian Episode" number two,' Freya whispered to Nicholas.

'Noted,' Nicholas answered.

'Freya, come and meet my sister,' Jolie ordered and she took Freya's arm and pulled her away from Nicholas. She led the way out of the glazed doors and towards a group of women on the patio area.

Freya held her breath as the cold wrapped around her.

'Lisa, this is Freya. Freya, this is my sister, Lisa,' Jolie introduced. A brown-haired woman of about her age smiled. She was dressed in a Cleopatra outfit.

'It's nice to meet you. Don't you two look alike,' Freya commented, visually comparing the two women.

'Everyone says that. I must be wearing well, I'm the eldest,' Lisa replied.

'Well whatever night cream you wear I'll endorse it.'

'Freya's a photographer, Lisa. She has her own studio in Carlton and the other week she took some risqué pictures of Kiefer Sutherland,' Jolie informed her.

'Oh my God! You know Kiefer Sutherland?!' Jennifer, one of the other women at the table shrieked. She was dressed in a Princess Leia outfit and her headdress almost fell off.

'Well, I wouldn't say I know him. I mean I met him last week for the photographs and he was really nice but we didn't do lunch or anything,' Freya told them.

'I love him. *24* was one of my favourite shows,' Jennifer said, her eyes glazing over.

'I suppose being engaged to Nicholas Kaden, you become kind of immune to celebrity,' Lisa suggested.

'I guess so. The thing is, I don't even think of Nick as a celebrity. He's just, you know, normal,' Freya said. She looked over to where Nicholas was helping Sam, Brian and Casey light the barbeque.

'Believe me, honey, there aren't many "normal" men on the planet that look as good as he does,' Lisa told her.

'Oh don't tell him that. I don't want him getting the idea that he's handsome or anything,' Freya joked with a smile.

'So, when are you two going to get married? Have you talked about a date yet? And where do you think you'll do it? You know if you live in Mayleaf you get to have a wedding in the square if you want it," Jolie said.

'Oh, we haven't really talked about a date. We're just so busy, there hasn't been time to think about it.'

She hadn't thought about it. Not at all. Was that strange? When she'd accepted his proposal she'd accepted because she wanted to spend the rest of her life with him, but the actual getting married part she hadn't really considered. What did she want and when did she want it?

She knew there was barely a gap in her diary for the next six months.

'I remember when Sam asked me to marry him. I said I wasn't going to get engaged to him until we'd set a date for the wedding. Long engagements are just a man's way of putting off the big day if you ask me,' Jolie remarked to the group.

'Well, we haven't had a long engagement yet. I mean, we've only been engaged six months or so,' Freya answered. Why did she feel like she had to justify why they hadn't set a date?

'Oh Freya, I wasn't meaning Nick was trying to put things off. Me and my big mouth! No, I just meant that for me a long engagement was out of the question. Well, I was pregnant with twins,' Jolie explained with a laugh.

'Are children something else we should have had by now?' Freya asked.

Their faces told her they weren't sure if she was joking. She laughed and they relaxed.

'My advice, leave off having kids for a few years. Your life's not your own once they're here,' Jolie said. The others at the table all nodded.

'Or better still, don't have them at all. They mess up your house and they don't understand the importance of not covering Mommy with sticky finger marks before she goes to work,' Lisa added.

'How old are your children?' Freya asked her.

'Seventeen and nineteen and the sticky hands and messy house still applies.'

Eight

It was gone midnight when the party drew to a close and everyone began to leave.

'Brian's asleep in the dog kennel, Sam. He can't stay there, he'll freeze to death,' Jolie told her husband as he said goodbye to his guests.

'Oh my God this is the fourth "Brian Episode" of the night! I'm just going to take a picture,' Freya announced. She hurried back through the house and out to the garden.

'Freya really does take photographs of everything, doesn't she?' Jolie remarked as Sam followed Freya in a bid to wake Brian up.

'Yes she does,' Nicholas replied with a smile.

'She's very talented. I saw the photographs she took of the Christian Fathers bridges. They're beautiful,' Jolie told him.

'She has a thing about those bridges. Some things she sees she just gets taken with and she kind of immerses herself in them. Put it this way, she gets more excited photographing those bridges than she did taking pictures of Kiefer Sutherland in the buff,' Nicholas tried to explain.

'An unnatural reaction I would say.'

'Unusual I admit, but I'm not sure the same would apply if it were Bruce Willis with no clothes on.'

Freya returned, a smile on her face and her small digital camera in her hand.

'You should have seen Brian. He had his head in Rusty's biscuit bowl and a bone in his hand.'

'Has Sam woken him up yet? I could really do without him staying over tonight. We have to be up early in the morning,' Jolie said, looking at her watch.

'Sam and Casey are going to walk him home to make sure he doesn't just pass out on the lawn outside,' Freya told her.

'We'll go, Jolie. Thank you for a great evening,' Nicholas said. He lent forward and kissed her on the cheek.

'Thank you both for coming. I'm sorry you got cornered by Sam's uncle Joe. He does like to talk,' Jolie said, kissing Freya's cheek.

'He advised me to get out of acting and into property development. He said that's where the real money is,' Nicholas said, smiling.

'Oh I'm sorry. He has no idea who you are,' Jolie spoke, sounding slightly embarrassed.

'I'm glad, particularly as I'm wearing this outfit.'

'Say goodbye to Sam for us and I'll probably see you later in the week,' Freya said. They left the house and started to walk down the path.

'Thanks again for coming. Take care getting home, it's almost freezing out there,' Jolie called.

Nicholas took hold of Freya's hand and they started out across town towards their home. It was certainly chilly and not the sort of weather to be outside for long when you were wearing flimsy fancy dress costumes.

'It was a nice evening,' Nicholas said.

'Yes it was and Jolie's sister is a real laugh. Apparently she lives a ten hour drive away. And there I was moaning about the flight times to Corfu,' Freya told him.

'Casey told me she's going through a divorce.'

'Really? She never mentioned it. That's sad.'

'Yeah, divorce is never nice even when it's amicable,' he agreed.

'Well I wouldn't know, having not been in that position.'

'Would you like to be?'

'Would I like to get divorced?'

'No! You know what I mean. Would you like to be in a position to get divorced? Would you like to be married?' Nicholas asked her. Despite the roundabout way this conversation had started, his tone was serious.

'Are you making me a proposition, Mr Kaden?' She smiled.

'I did that in Corfu remember? But, perhaps now's the time to reaffirm that intention,' he suggested.

'Has Sam been talking to you about long engagements?' Freya queried.

'Sam? No. What made you ask that?'

'Because Jolie asked me tonight if we'd set a date for the wedding. When I told her we hadn't, she said she didn't believe in long engagements or indefinite engagements,' Freya explained.

'Well, I think I have to agree with her.'

'You do?'

'Yes, I think we should set a date.'

'But when? I mean you're off filming in Africa soon for four months and I'm up to my eyes working on the Every Day project. I just can't see us having time to organise a wedding.'

'We can make time, Freya. I mean, for all the work we both do, charity or otherwise, we still have to have time for us,' he reminded her.

'I know but…' Freya started.

'Have you changed your mind about wanting to marry me?'

He stopped walking and turned to face her.

'No. God, Nick no. Don't be stupid,' she exclaimed, taking hold of both his hands and squeezing them tight.

'Then what is it? What's freaking you out about setting a date for our wedding?'

'Oh I don't know. The thought of planning it all probably. I mean weddings are about families and I don't have one. That kind of means your side of the church is going to be packed full of people and mine is going to have the Petroholis family,' Freya said, sighing.

'I haven't exactly got a big family, Freya. Anyway, if we invite all the Petroholis family, including all their aunts, uncles and cousins we'll need to hire the entire Empire State Building for the reception.'

Freya smiled. He was right. Once that Greek family got together it was like a crowd inside a baseball game.

'And it takes a lot of organisation, which is fine if you're Emma, but not so good if you're me. I mean, I couldn't organise a personal organiser,' Freya told him.

'So, do you want a lavish white wedding with ten bridesmaids and a team of coordinators? Or were you planning to sell the rights to the photographs to *Shooting Stars* magazine?' Nicholas asked her.

'Well, no.'

'Then what's the problem? Let's set a date and plan the wedding we want. A quiet wedding if that's what you'd prefer,' he suggested.

'But is that what *you* want too? It isn't just about me.'

'I want whatever you want, Freya. I just want to make a commitment to you. I want you to be my wife. How we make the commitment isn't so important as long as it's special, for both of us.'

'So, if I said I wanted to just fly to Las Vegas one day and get married in a drive-through chapel with two witnesses and an Elvis impersonator you would be cool with that?'

'Yes I would. If it means making you Mrs Kaden I'd be cool with anything,' he told her.

She nodded and then turned away from him and began walking across the street towards the road to their home.

'So? Is that the end of the conversation? Do you need time to think about it or something?' He hurried to catch her up.

'No one's been able to tell me if we're going to get snow here. Do you think a winter wedding would be cool?'

'You want to do it now? Near Christmas?' The excitement in his voice was clear.

'Yes, is that too soon for you? I thought that if we're going to do it, we'd better do it before you go all *Out of Africa* on me.'

'A winter wedding sounds fantastic. Come here,' he ordered her. He took hold of her arm and pulled her towards him.

Looking down at her, he gently ran his fingers across the surgeon's headscarf covering her forehead. He cupped her face with his hands. Freya smiled at him and put her arms around his neck, pulling him towards her to kiss him.

'I love you, Freya.'

'I love you too.'

He kissed her nose and slipped his hand into hers.

'So do you really want to go to Vegas?' he asked.

'I haven't decided how I want to do it yet. But one thing I do know...*I'm* going to be the one wearing the dress.' She pulled at the hem of Nicholas' nurse uniform and ran off up the road laughing.

Nine

Elvis was singing to her. It was 'Love me Tender' and he was dressed in a white flared jumpsuit covered in rhinestones. His hair was jet black, styled in a quiff and he was wearing huge gold sunglasses. And then her nose felt wet and scratchy. It was like someone was rubbing a damp emery board across it.

Freya opened her eyes and felt fur touch her cheek and whiskers poke her eyes. It was Willis, licking her nose.

'You hungry?' Freya asked him.

She turned on her side, trying not to make Willis topple from the bed and reached for her glasses on the nightstand. She caught sight of the time on the clock radio. It was almost seven thirty.

'Daddy up early again, Willis? Come on, let's go and get you some breakfast and see what he's up to,' Freya said. She stroked the cat's head.

She got out of bed, tied her robe around her and headed out of the bedroom. Willis skipped in front of her and led the way down the stairs.

The door leading to the basement was open. That meant Nicholas was working out. Converting the cellar into a state of the art gym was the only modification they'd made to the house since moving in. Freya knew he found it tiresome, but keeping himself in shape was essential for Nicholas' profession. When the equipment was first installed, she'd attempted to have a turn on the running machine. She soon found out it wasn't an activity you could multitask on. She had nearly choked on a chocolate muffin and almost scalded herself with a hot cup of tea. She hadn't been near the equipment since.

Willis weaved in and out of her legs as she negotiated the stairs down to the gym. Nicholas was seated, his back to her, bare from the waist up, using the lateral pull-down.

Freya stood and watched him. He had an amazing physique she could look at all day. She quickly pulled a small digital camera out of the pocket of her robe and snapped a couple of pictures.

'Hey,' he greeted. He let go of the weights and turned around to face her.

'Morning. So, at what hour did you decide you'd rather spend time with these boring, ugly, stiff machines instead of me?' Freya asked, walking towards him, Willis hot on her heels.

'It was about six, or just after. I woke and I couldn't get back to sleep and I thought if I do this now I won't have to do it later. I thought maybe we could go out to dinner tonight.' He stood up, reached for his towel and rubbed his face with it.

'My choice?'

'Yeah, why not. I've just about recovered from the last feeding frenzy we went on when we did four different restaurants in the one evening.'

Willis let out a miaow and jumped up on to the stepper machine. It started to move and scared him. He leapt off and raced up the cellar steps.

'Willis is hungry and so am I. Have you eaten?' Freya asked. She took the towel from him and rubbed the sweat from his back.

'No, what have we got?'

'The leftover pizza's still there. It's probably still good for one more day. Or there's a carton of Chinese we didn't finish on Tuesday. Or there are blueberry muffins from the diner but they've been hanging around a while so perhaps they ought to go in the bin,' Freya recounted as they made their way back up to the main house.

'Do we not have bread and eggs or cereal?'

'Well yeah, we have those things. But they aren't very exciting.'

'I'm making scrambled eggs with toast and I'm putting all that leftover takeaway food in the trash,' he told her.

'The "bin" God damn it! The "bin"! Even the pizza? It's got everything on it.'

'Especially the pizza. If it's been around that long it's got everything on it and a whole lot more.'

Willis was sat on the kitchen counter when they arrived in the room, rubbing his head against the cupboard housing his food.

'So, you haven't forgotten what we're doing today have you?' Nicholas asked.

'Do we have something planned?'

'The new scanning equipment's going to be used for the first time at Carlton General Hospital today. We're doing a meet and greet with the patients, cutting a ribbon and having lunch with the hospital board. You really had forgotten, hadn't you?'

'Oh God is that today?! Yes, I had forgotten, but that's fine. I'll call Sasha, have her check the diary and cancel anything I might have stupidly put in. I did say I wasn't an organiser,' Freya reminded him.

And Nicholas definitely hadn't told her. His assistant probably sent her a bossy email and she probably deleted it.

'Well, while you're on the phone to her you can ask her to check appointments for next month and then we can make a firm date for the wedding.'

'I will.'

'No second thoughts this morning then?' Nicholas asked her. He cracked some eggs into a pan.

'No, but I had a rather terrifying dream about an Elvis impersonator. Hey, did you make tea for the photographers when you got up?' Freya asked.

'No. I looked out and there was only one guy there and I didn't recognise him.'

'Well Donny will be there by now. I'll make a pot.'

'You are crazy, you know that, don't you?' He shook his head at her.

'And that makes you crazy for wanting to marry me.'

The phone rang and Nicholas crossed the kitchen to pick up the cordless handset stationed on the wall.

'Hello…oh hi Sasha. That's OK…I'm fine thank you and you? That's good…yeah…uh huh…well that was good thinking…'

'Hey, does she want to speak to me at all? Her boss?' Freya asked.

'Freya's right here. Yeah, I'll put her on…yes OK, I will,' Nicholas said. He held out the receiver for Freya to take.

'Hello.'

'Hi, Freya, I'm sorry to bother you at home this early but I wanted to remind you about your visit to Carlton General today. I meant to mention it yesterday but

I had my meeting with Heather Malcolm and it went right out of my head.'

'That's OK. My fiancé is thankfully better organised than me and he also has a PA who emails lots of intricate looking schedules. But thank you for reminding me. Have I got anything else booked in for this afternoon?' Freya wanted to know.

'No, but there's a message from Jonathan Sanders on the answer phone suggesting he meet you for lunch tomorrow to discuss the plan he put to you yesterday. He was a little vague.'

'Jonny,' Freya said out loud.

'Shall I call him back to accept or did you want to do that?' Sasha questioned.

'Sasha, are you in the office right now?' Freya asked. She moved from the kitchen out into the hallway.

'Er, yes I am.'

'Sasha, it's not even eight. What are you doing there? Don't you have a bed to be in? Or someone else's bed to be in?' Freya asked her.

'Well, Heather Malcolm accepted my proposal for the college football photographs so I wanted to make a start with the organisation.'

'Sasha, why can't I be as efficient as you?'

'I…' Sasha started.

'This afternoon we'll do what I said yesterday. We'll turn off the phones and get stuck into something. Maybe we'll go out somewhere and take some pictures,' Freya suggested to her.

'I'd really like that.'

'Good. Well, while you're on the phone and in the office, could you check the diary for next month and see when I have some free time? I'll need a week or so clear,' Freya said.

'You're pretty busy. There are meetings about the Every Day project, but there is a reasonably clear week at the end of the month. There are one or two appointments but...' Sasha began.

'You mean around Christmas.'

'Yes.'

'Could you cancel those appointments? And give me the date of one of the Saturdays either end of that week,' Freya asked her.

'Twenty second?'

'Great. That's perfect. Right, well could you book me out that Saturday and the whole of the following week?'

'Are you taking a vacation?'

'"Holiday", Sasha. Yes I am, a honeymoon.' She smiled to herself. A honeymoon.

'Oh. Well, that's great, congratulations.'

'Thank you. Well, I shall see you a bit later and if Milo at the patisserie has any new recipes he'd like me to try out, save me something for this afternoon,' Freya finished.

'Sure. See you.'

Freya returned to the kitchen and replaced the phone on the wall.

'Everything OK?' Nicholas asked. He buttered toast.

'Everything's fine. In fact you'd better call your brother later and make sure he can get here for the twenty second of December.'

'You've decided on a date.' He turned to face her.

'Can you make it?'

'I think I'm supposed to be meeting with Arnold Schwarzenegger that day, but I'm sure he'll understand,' Nicholas replied, slipping his arms around her waist.

'Tell him *you'll be back*,' Freya suggested with a laugh.

'I'll tell him I can't meet him because I'm going to be made the happiest man alive.'

'You'll make me blush and you know I hate blushing in front of Willis.'

'He's gotten used to it. Come on, let's eat breakfast and then I'll call Matt, tell him the good news.' He let her go and picked up the plates from the work top.

Twenty second of December. She was going to be a winter bride. Now the date was set she had to think about what she wanted and where she wanted it. Where did she start?

'So, who's Jonny?' Nicholas asked, sitting down at the table.

'Jonny?'

She swallowed. She should have told him yesterday. Whatever she told him now, after the event, was going to sound lame. Unless she lied to buy time. Why did she need to lie? There was nothing between her and Jonny.

'Yeah, Sasha said something to you on the phone and you said *Jonny* in kind of a weird way.'

'Oh, Jonny! *That* Jonny! Oh, that's Sasha's latest guy. He's nothing to write home about and if you ask me she could do a lot better than him. He stood her up last week with no good excuse.'

There was the lie, tripping from her tongue. She sat at the table with a thump.

'She seems quite a nice girl. She certainly likes to talk.'

'She is nice and talented. Obviously not as talented as me, but I'm trying to pass on a few things to her,' Freya told him.

'So, December twenty second.' He looked across the table at her, a smile on his face.

'Yep, twenty second of December, it's a date.'

If God didn't smite her for the lying.

Ten

The car arrived to pick them up at ten. Roger, Nicholas' bodyguard, arrived in it. As much as Freya liked raising money for charity, she absolutely hated the meet and greets. Meeting the people was fine, she loved talking. But being photographed from every conceivable angle and being asked endless questions by journalists was her idea of hell. Even though she had endured months of it already, she still didn't seem to get any better at it. She slightly envied Nicholas' relaxed demeanor in dealing with it all. He was excellent at being amiable to anybody and everybody.

Another reason Freya disliked public functions was the fact she felt she had to consider carefully what she wore. Too formal and she would be thought of as too business-like, too casual and she would be seen as not serious enough. It was a nightmare. Usually she didn't care what people thought, but the charity work was important to her. Today she had opted for a smart grey trouser suit and a black shirt.

'Hi, Roger,' Freya greeted, hurrying down the steps to embrace him.

'Hey, Freya. How you doing?' He hugged her.

'I'm good. Really good.' She couldn't stop the smile from spreading across her face.

'I know that look, you have something going on.'

'We might have. Nick, Roger thinks we have something going on. Do you want to tell him or shall I?' Freya called as Nicholas appeared at the front door. He was looking every inch the Hollywood heartthrob in a charcoal grey suit.

'We've set a date for the wedding, Roger. December twenty second.' Nicholas took Freya's hand in his.

'Well, that is fantastic news. Congratulations, man,' Roger said. He held his hand out to his boss.

'Thanks, Roger.'

'And it goes without saying we would really love you and Dionne to be there. In fact, Roger, I kind of need you to do something else as well,' Freya spoke in serious tones.

'I'll wait in the car,' Nicholas said. He winked at Freya and opened the door.

'You want me to organise the security?' Roger asked.

'No, God no! I'm hoping we can do this quietly and without the need for anything like that. No, I was rather hoping you might give me away.'

'My, I wasn't expecting that. I don't know what to say.'

Freya watched him fiddle with the collar of his shirt.

'Well, you know my history with my father, *and* my mother for that matter. And you know, since we share the same admiration of Bruce Willis, I thought it was a good enough reason to ask you,' Freya continued.

'Freya, I would be truly honoured to give you away.'

'You would?! Well that's great!' She threw her arms around him and hugged him close. They'd formed a bond from the moment they'd met and he was the closest thing she had to a father figure.

'Any idea on location yet?' he asked.

'I have a few ideas and I'm not telling you any of them. Because I know if I tell you, you'll be mentally working out where all the exits are.'

'You know me way too well.'

Half an hour later the car pulled up outside Carlton General Hospital and Freya could see the whole state's photographers and journalists were outside waiting to take photographs and ask questions.

'I really, really hate this,' Freya remarked to Nicholas as they prepared to get out of the car.

'I know you do and you know I would rather go in through the back door. But it's publicity the charity needs to ensure its future,' he reminded her.

'Yes I know, I know. I just would rather come here at the dead of night and speak to people privately, not pose for the papers.'

She also had the beginnings of a spot on her nose and although she'd concealed, those lenses were unforgiving.

'It'll be fine and remember there's a meal waiting for us after we've done the posing and the smiling and all the publicity shots.'

'I know, that thought will see me through. OK, let's go.'

They got out of the car and the photography began at once. There were whirrs and clicks coming from all directions and Freya gritted her teeth and smiled, holding on tight to Nicholas' hand.

'Freya, Nick, over here!'

'Freya, Nick, how does it feel to know that the people of Carlton and the surrounding towns will benefit from advanced cancer screening thanks to your donations?' another journalist yelled in their direction.

'Both Freya and I are delighted that we've been able to obtain this equipment for Carlton General and we hope it will end up saving many lives,' Nicholas answered.

'Freya, may I be the first to offer my congratulations on setting the wedding date.'

The voice calling out from behind them had Freya spinning round to see who was speaking. There she was, Sandra McNeill from *Shooting Stars* magazine. They had met on more than one occasion, the first being when Freya met Nicholas in Corfu.

'Sorry, Sandra, what did you say?' Freya asked.

'December twenty second, the date for your wedding. Will you be going back to England or having a ceremony in Hollywood?' Sandra continued, her recorder held out.

'Nick, are you hearing this?' Freya asked him, pulling on his hand.

'Sandra, I'm afraid you've yet again found yourself an unreliable source. Freya and I haven't set a date for our wedding yet, but when we do you will be the first to know.'

Nicholas directed Freya away from Sandra McNeill and towards the entrance of the hospital where the board members were waiting to meet them.

'She knew the date of our wedding. We've told three people and she knew. How?' Freya wanted to know.

'You know what it's like. News like that just has a habit of getting out. We have a team of photographers permanently at our front gate. Maybe they overheard you talking to Roger,' Nicholas suggested.

'Our gate is nearly one hundred yards from our front door, Nick. They couldn't have overheard,' Freya whispered.

'Hey, calm down, it isn't the end of the world. It was going to get out sooner or later, it's the nature of the beast. Don't let it get to you, you know what reporters are like. They could probably track down your "Wild Wednesday" pants if they put their minds to it.' He smiled and squeezed her hand.

'Do you think our house is bugged?' Freya asked.

'Now you're being ridiculous and you really have to cut down the amount of crime dramas you watch,' he responded with a laugh.

'I don't like people knowing things like that when we've only just decided it ourselves.'

It wasn't just irritating it was unnerving. She didn't want to think anyone she'd told about the wedding date would divulge the information to someone like Sandra McNeill.

'Listen, don't let it spoil how we feel about setting the date. People are bound to be interested, but at the end of the day it's our private event. So they can talk about it all they like, but they won't be getting invitations.'

Freya nodded but Sandra McNeill's comment had unsettled her. She was just getting used to the idea herself, the last thing she wanted was to have the moment ruined.

It was still playing on Freya's mind when they were being given a tour of one of the cancer wards by Bill Stanton, the chairman of the hospital.

'Nick, Freya, this is Katherine. She hasn't been able to stop talking about you coming to visit since we told her about it,' Bill Stanton introduced as they stopped walking and stood at the foot of one of the beds.

A pale, dark-haired, dark-eyed girl of approximately eight years old lay in the bed they had halted at. She looked pale and frail and was attached to a drip.

'Hi, Katherine,' Nicholas greeted. He went closer to her and sat on the edge of her bed.

'Hi…you are my favourite actor. I think you're cool,' Katherine spoke quietly. She attempted to sit herself up.

'Well thank you very much. Katherine, this is Freya, my fiancée,' he introduced. He motioned Freya to come nearer to the bed.

'Hi, Katherine, it's very nice to meet you. Do you know, he's my favourite actor too,' Freya said, smiling.

'Freya! How can you lie to Katherine like that? Freya's favourite actor is Bruce Willis.'

'I like him too. What's a fiancée?' Katherine questioned.

'Well, being someone's fiancée means you're going to get married to that person one day. Freya and I are going to get married,' he told the girl.

'Wow! Are you going to have a big white dress and bridesmaids and a fancy cake?' Katherine asked. At the mention of a wedding she had perked up and was overflowing with excitement.

'Well, I'm not quite sure yet, maybe. Is that what you'd like when you get married one day?' Freya asked her.

'If I was getting married I'd have five bridesmaids. My mom, my sister, Karen and my friends Anne, Britney and Erica. And I would make my daddy wear a real smart suit so he would look nice when he took me to the church,' Katherine explained, a faraway look in her eyes.

'That sounds like a perfect wedding day to me,' Freya said, smiling.

'Is your daddy going to wear a smart suit to your wedding?' Katherine asked, looking directly at Freya with her huge brown eyes.

'My daddy,' Freya repeated the words.

Her pulse quickened and she had to take a breath.

'Um, Katherine, Freya's father can't come to our wedding, but we are going to make sure all of our friends are there to help us make it a special day,' Nicholas interjected quickly.

'Why can't your daddy come?' Katherine continued. Her sorrowful eyes seemed to be getting larger and more questioning by the second.

'Well, because...' Nicholas began.

'Because he died,' Freya interrupted.

'Oh,' Katherine replied. She seemed satisfied with the answer.

'Say, that nice man over there is going to take our photo,' Nicholas said, indicating the photographer hired for the publicity shots.

Freya got up and left Nicholas and Katherine. She went across the ward to Bill Stanton who was talking to one of the nurses on duty.

'Hey, Bill, tell me. What are Katherine's chances of recovery?' She watched Nicholas with Katherine. He had his arms around her, hugging her close.

'She has acute myeloid leukaemia. She's already had a bone marrow transplant and extensive chemotherapy.'

'She's going to die?' Bill's tone had been clear but Freya couldn't believe it. She didn't want to believe it.

'Yes,' he responded.

'But she's only a kid.' This was so unfair. 'How long?'

'It's likely to be weeks rather than months,' Bill answered.

She felt sick. She had had countless similar moments at hospitals all over the state, but she still wasn't immune to the shock when the reality of the situation hit home. There she was, concerned about people knowing her wedding date, when there was an eight year old child losing her fight for life and talking enthusiastically about a wedding she would never grow up to have.

Freya's eyes glazed over with tears as Nicholas came back to rejoin her.

'You OK?' he asked. He put his arm around her, held her close.

'She only has weeks to live. Weeks, Nick,' Freya stated. She felt hopeless and helpless.

'I know.'

'But it's horrible and unfair and God, I don't think I can stomach a lunch after this. I think I want to go home and cry.'

'Hey, come on, put on a brave face for Katherine and all the other people here. Maybe there's nothing we can do to save *her*, but there are hundreds of people we *are* helping by providing this equipment,' he reminded her.

'Nick, when I complain about stuff, I don't know, like if the post is late or Sadie Fox has cancelled me or someone's pissed me off driving like an idiot on the motorway. Will you tell me how lucky I am and remind me of this moment?'

'Sure, you bet.' He squeezed her hand and kissed her on the cheek.

Eleven

The lunch with the board members of the hospital took longer than anticipated and it was almost three in the afternoon before Freya arrived at her studio.

When she entered the building Sasha appeared, holding out a brown paper bag.

'Chocolate fudge brownie with real cherry pieces,' Sasha announced.

'Oh, Sasha, it sounds fantastic but I'm absolutely stuffed. The dinner was four courses,' Freya said. She swallowed some rising indigestion.

'Well, take it for later.' She shook the bag.

'OK, thanks. Right, so, shall we get ready to go out? Before I sit in my chair and pass out,' Freya suggested. She crossed the hall and opened the door to one of the studios.

'Are you sure you have time? I mean...' Sasha began.

'Yes I have time. Don't you want to go?' She pulled out some black leather cases and put them in the hallway.

'Oh no I *really* want to go, I just don't want to impose on your time that's all,' Sasha told her.

'Don't be stupid, Sasha. Get your gear and let's get out of here.' Freya smiled, put the bags over her shoulder and walked back towards the door.

It didn't take long to put all the equipment in the back of Freya's SUV and soon the two women were on their way out of town.

'How did the hospital visit go?' Sasha asked as Freya drove.

'It was OK. Well, it was sad actually, but then it's always sad. We met this little girl called Katherine. She's got leukaemia. She's only got weeks to live and she's so small and pretty and sweet. It was heartbreaking,' Freya admitted.

She hadn't been able to shake the image of Katherine from her mind. Life was cruel.

'But it must be heartwarming to know you'll be saving other lives by donating so much to the Carlton hospital and to the cancer charities,' Sasha spoke.

'That's exactly what Nick said and I know he's right. But it doesn't stop it being unjust and terribly sad.'

'No. So, are you and Nick going to have your photograph in the paper again this week?'

'Yes, unfortunately. Still, at least on this occasion it's for a good cause.'

'I think what you do is amazing. It's fantastic that someone as busy as Nick takes time out to help other people. It's so selfless.' Sasha looked out the window.

'Yes it is,' Freya agreed.

It was only a short drive to County Bridge and when they got there Freya parked at the side of the road and jumped out to unload the car.

'Wow, it's cold. Glad I brought a jacket. Are they expecting snow?' Freya asked.

'I like snow.'

'To look at, yes. To live with, not so much.'

'Here, let me help you...I didn't realise we were going to come here,' Sasha said, taking a case from Freya.

'Have you been to this bridge before?'

'No, I just recognised it from your photographs. Do you know why they're painted black?' Sasha put a bag over her shoulder.

'Well, I've heard several stories about that. They range from a mistake when the paint was ordered and no funds to change it, to it representing death and reincarnation.'

'I heard that the only birds living around here are crows. That can't be true can it?'

They began to walk across the grassland towards the bridge.

'Well, I can honestly say they're the only birds *I've* seen here.'

'Don't you think that's strange?'

'Maybe, I don't know. But, what I *do* know is the combination of the dark bridge with the muddy water, the tall grass and the uninterrupted view of the skyline is just about as perfect as you're going to get and it's a great place to practise,' Freya told her.

They set up the equipment and Freya looked through the camera at the scene in front of her.

'So, Sasha, why d'you think I've chosen this particular camera? It's one of my Canons, that's a clue.'

'Well, maybe because it's an analogue camera and these scenes will definitely look better using film. Um, it has a seven point wide area auto focus, that should help with getting a good balance between the foreground, the background and the subject of the picture. And, I believe it has manual dioptric adjustment.'

'Sometimes you really concern me, Sasha. The answer of course is because it has a funky name, Rebel, and because it looks cute. But I suppose your answers were right too. OK, get behind the camera and tell me what you see,' Freya urged her.

Sasha put her face to the viewfinder and looked through the camera.

'I would say we need to zoom in a little if we want to make the bridge the centrepiece of the shot,' Sasha said.

'OK, that's one idea. But why don't you have another look and perhaps you'll see something that might be a more unusual centrepiece,' Freya suggested.

'Oh God, I nearly didn't see it at all! There's a tiny boat moored at the edge of the bank. It's white so it's a perfect contrast to the bridge.' The assistant's excitement was evident.

'You got it. So, shoot away, I've bought plenty of film,' Freya said. She stepped away from Sasha and took her mobile phone out of her handbag.

She pressed a key and put it to her ear.

'Hello,' Emma answered.

Her friend sounded more exhausted than the last time they had spoken.

'Hi Em, how you doing? How's Melly?' She sat down and made herself comfortable on the grass.

'Oh hi, Freya. She's not very well today. She keeps being sick.'

'Oh no. Have you seen the doctor?'

'Yes, he hasn't long left. He thinks she probably has a bug, but she can't keep anything down. We're having to make sure she at least has some water at regular intervals. The doctor's coming back tonight to see how she is.'

'Oh poor Melly and poor you.'

'Yeah, I'm exhausted and Yiannis has been up all night too.'

'Well, I won't keep you long and feel free to dive off and mop up puke if you need to. Nick and I have set a date for the wedding and I wanted you to be one of the first couple of thousand people to know.'

The knowledge that Sandra McNeill knew the news before the best friend still sickened her.

'Oh, Freya! How exciting! When? And what do you mean one of the first couple of thousand?' Emma queried.

'Well, believe it or not, I told two people and Nick told his brother and somehow Sandra McNeill found out. At this moment the witch is broadcasting it to the entire world. It's the twenty second of December.'

'Twenty second of December. Well, that gives you over a year. That's plenty of time to plan.'

'Yes, well it would if it were twenty second of December *next* year.'

'What? Oh my God! You mean it's next month?! Are you crazy? You can't plan a wedding in that amount of time! We planned mine in less than seven months and it was touch and go whether the dress would be ready on time,' Emma reminded her.

'Well, we don't want a big wedding. We just want something small and uncomplicated with just us and the people we care about.'

'You mean you could afford the most lavish ceremony anyone could think of and you aren't going to make the most of that?'

'Em! All that pomp and extravagance just because I can afford it?! You know that isn't me.'

'I know you detest wasting money but sometimes a little bit of luxury, particularly for your wedding day, isn't greed.'

'We've discussed it, neither of us wants that. I can't imagine anything worse than saying my vows and being drowned out by Channel Nine trying to take photographs from a helicopter.'

She could picture the scene. Sandra McNeill would be harnessed up and hanging out, a notepad in one hand, a voice recorder in the other.

'So, have you talked about where you might do it? Are you going to get married in church?'

'I don't know. Nick got married in church the first time and I don't know why, but every time I walk into a church I get the feeling I'm going to start spurting ectoplasm or disintegrate if I get splashed by holy water.'

'You survived *my* wedding.'

'I did. But if you remember, I did tell you I had a close encounter with the cross on the altar when I was fruitlessly searching for your flowers. No, I don't think a church. Apparently, 'cause we live in Mayleaf we can get married in the town square if we want to.' Freya turned her attention to Sasha, watching her take the camera off the tripod and move closer to the water.

'And would you want to?' Emma asked.

'Well, it does have the advantage of the protection of the Town Circle. That works like some invisible cyber cordon keeping away anyone who has any connection with the media.'

'And what are your other options?'

'Well, Las Vegas if I fancy sharing our big day with a couple of thousand fruit machines and a couple of hundred Elvises. Or should that be Elvi? Is that the plural?'

'Las Vegas. At one of those tiny little chapels where you get married in seconds and could get divorced even quicker?'

'What's good enough for Britney Spears is good enough for me.'

'Why don't you get married here?' Emma suggested.

'In Corfu?'

'Why not? You met each other here. You got back together here. Nick proposed to you here. Why not get married here? It doesn't have to be in the church. You could probably get married at Villa Kamia, right here where I'm standing in the garden.'

There was definite excitement in Emma's voice.

'How cold is it there right now? Are you expecting snow?'

'I don't think so.'

'It's sounding appealing.'

'Well, I think it's a great idea and I bet Nick would love it. I mean, you could even stay on and have your honeymoon here. No extravagance because you have the villa already, as little media attention as you're going to get and you get to meet Melly and see me and Yiannis again.'

'God, that sounds so tempting.'

'It would be perfect!'

'Well let's hold the thought and I'll speak to Nick about it tonight.'

She watched Sasha move down the bank, towards the river, then lost sight of her.

'What did Nick say about Jonny?' Emma wanted to know.

'Oh, well I haven't really had time to talk to him about it. We went to the hospital today because it was the first day the new scanning equipment was going to be used and...' Freya began.

'Freya, you *have* to tell him. You can't have secrets from each other, particularly now, when you're planning your marriage. He'll be hurt if you don't tell him and he finds out from someone like Sandra McNeill.'

'I know, I *will* tell him. I'm going to tell him. I'm going to tell him tonight.'

'What are you so worried about? What d'you think he's going to say?'

'I don't know. It's just stepping back into that past life again when I have *so* moved on. I don't want it to upset things.'

'Freya, got to go. Melly's been sick again. I'll call you later.'

Freya put her phone away and stood up. She rubbed her cold hands together and went in search of Sasha.

She found her at the edge of the riverbank, the camera trained on the other side.

'No fishermen today. There are usually a couple of them fishing a little up river about this time,' Freya remarked.

'Oh, Freya, you startled me. I was so engrossed in what I was doing.' Sasha turned around to face her.

'That's OK, I get like that a lot. A herd of cattle could come running by and I wouldn't notice. So, how did you get on?'

'Well, I've nearly finished the roll but I guess we won't see the result until we get into the dark room.'

'Right, well shall we take some pictures from on the bridge? You can just about see Riley's Hill from there,' Freya said.

She picked up a bag and led the way.

Twelve

That evening Freya decided they were going to attempt the Mayleaf Round Robin. That meant having something at all of Mayleaf's eateries. Although Mayleaf was a small town it had a Chinese takeaway, a diner, a barbecue restaurant, a hot dog stand near Sam and Jolie's store and a pizza parlour.

'We really shouldn't even be considering this, Freya. We had four courses at lunch time,' Nicholas reminded her as they walked towards the Chinese takeaway.

The temperature had dropped a good few degrees and the clear, star-filled sky was a sign of a frost to come. At the moment it was actually too cold for snow.

'I know, but I thought about this. I decided if we have really small, tiny, little portions at each place it would probably be less filling than ordering one huge main course at Casey's,' Freya replied.

'I'm not entirely sure that logic works but I'm willing to give it a go.' He pushed open the door of the Chinese.

'Hey, Bruce, how are you?' Freya greeted the owner of the takeaway.

Bruce stood no more than five feet tall. It meant he had to stand on a box to see over the counter to serve people. He had thinning dark hair, a big smile and always had a pencil tucked behind his ear. Freya had never seen him use it.

'Freya and Nick, good evening to you both.' Bruce smiled, bowed, then leapt on to his box so he could see them properly.

'Hi, Bruce, how you doing? How's Li?' Nicholas asked. Li was Bruce's wife.

'She is fine. In the kitchen, where a good woman should always be,' he answered with a wry smile.

'God, Bruce, you really know how to hit the spot don't you! If I thought you really meant that and if I knew I could get spring rolls like yours somewhere else, I would boycott your place,' Freya told him.

'You are lucky man, Nick, lucky man.' He laughed as he picked up his order book.

'I know,' Nicholas replied, looking to Freya.

'Right, we'll have a portion of spring rolls and some satay chicken. Oh and some sweet and sour pork and chuck in some prawn crackers,' Freya ordered.

'Hey, I thought we were only having small, tiny portions.'

'We are. I'm ordering breakfast for the next couple of days.' She grinned.

'It will be 'bout fifteen minutes.'

'Great, we'll call back,' Freya said.

'Call back? Where are we going?'

'To Sam and Jolie's to get a bottle of wine to go with our Chinese. I thought we could eat in the gazebo. We've wrapped up toasty. It isn't the four courses under here, I've got three layers under this jacket.'

Twenty minutes later they were sat cross-legged in the gazebo in the town square, tucking into the Chinese food and sharing a straw to drink the bottle of white wine they'd bought.

'You would have thought Sam and Jolie would've stocked up on plastic glasses by now. This has to be the fourth or fifth occasion we've drunk wine through a straw,' Freya remarked as she took her turn with the bottle.

'I'm more surprised you don't carry some in your bag - along with the two cameras and the Blu Tack.'

'And didn't the Blu Tack come in handy when the hem of your trousers unraveled that time.'

'Bottle please. It's definitely my turn.' He held his hand out for the wine.

Freya took a bite of her spring roll and watched Nicholas as he sucked on the straw. She was trying to wait for exactly the right moment to bring up Jonny. But she knew better than anyone that right moments never came. You had to face things head on and just get it out there.

'Nick,' she began.

'Yeah.'

'There's something I have to tell you.'

'Oh? Am I going to need to suck a bit harder on this straw to soften the blow?'

'Possibly.'

'Go on,' he urged.

'You remember I told you about Jonathan, the boy I went out with when I was seventeen.'

'Of course I remember. You were in love with him. You told him who you were and took him to meet your folks and they welcomed him with open arms only for your father to pay him money to leave you alone,' Nicholas recounted.

'Yes, you obviously don't have a problem with your memory. That was about the size of it.' She let out a nervous sigh. She didn't know why she was nervous. There was nothing to this, absolutely nothing.

'What about him?'

'Well, I met him. Yesterday. He lives here now, in America.' She'd said it quick before she backed out.

'*He's* Jonny.' He put the bottle of wine down and sat up straight.

'Yes. He's Jonny,' she admitted.

'So, he isn't the Jonny Sasha's dating? That's a different Jonny is it?'

'Yes. Well, actually Sasha isn't exactly dating anyone called Jonny.' Her face was red and she couldn't look at Nicholas. She sounded like an infant lying and trying to cover it up very unsuccessfully. And what was the big deal anyway? Nothing was going on.

'No? You surprise me. Why didn't you tell me, Freya?'

His expression was a mixture of angry and sad. Why hadn't she told him straight away? Why had she kept it to herself?

'Oh, I don't know. It felt awkward and I didn't want you to think what I *thought* you would think.'

'And what did you think I would think?'

'I don't know. Maybe that I was hiding something from you I suppose.'

'Which you were. Freya, are you saying you were too scared to tell me because you were worried about what I'd think?'

'No. Yes. I don't know what I thought. He's just from my past. That horrible, awful past and I don't want things from back then to be part of our future.'

'Neither do I, but that shouldn't mean you don't tell me stuff. We're about to get married. We should be able to share everything with each other.' He got to his feet and picked his jacket up from the floor.

'We do. I've told you everything, except this. And I'm telling you now. Nick, please, sit down. I'm sorry.' She stood up and tried to take hold of his arm. He brushed it away.

'Back in Corfu, we said no more secrets and I meant that.' He folded his arms across his chest.

'I meant it too. It was stupid not to tell you about Jonny, I realise that now. In fact I realised it the minute I thought it was too late to mention it. Then, as time went on, I realised more and more how stupid it was. But, you know now.'

She sounded pathetic. There was no justification for it.

'Well, what did he want? You haven't really told me anything yet.'

'Will you sit down and help me out with the sweet and sour pork?' She gave him half a smile, wary of his reaction.

'What did he want, Freya?' Nicholas repeated, unmoved.

'He wants to develop some land near Gatebrook and turn it into a community for the Every Day project. Housing, jobs, a school.' She rattled it out fast.

Nicholas didn't reply. He remained standing, his arms crossed, looking down at Freya.

'He's a property developer now. He owns the chain, Recuperation Inns, amongst other things. He's changed so much - in appearance, in personality - I hardly recognised him.'

'So, let me get this straight. This Jonny turns up...where? At your office? At our house? And he pledges millions of pounds to your charity. I don't get it. Why would he do that?'

'He told me he thought the project was a great idea. But I also think he was feeling a little guilty about how he treated me.'

'I'm sorry, Freya. I don't buy it.'

'What d'you mean? He told me he made a bid on some land I've bought for the first centre in Chesterville and he found out I was behind the project.'

'How?'

'How what?'

'How did he find out you were behind the project?'

'I don't know. He said he had contacts and...'

'Whoa!'

'He wants to support the charity.'

'But what's in it for him? If he's turned into some big shot hotel owner and property developer, why does he want to throw money at your charity?'

Freya could almost see the steam coming out of his ears. He didn't get angry often, but when he did it wasn't pleasant.

'Well, you could say the same about us. And anyway, why does *anyone* give to charity? Maybe to do something for someone else. Or get rid of some excess cash so the tax man doesn't get it. Or perhaps they do it because it makes them feel good or look good to other people. I don't know, maybe he wants to make himself feel better about building those ugly hotels all over the place.'

'OK, let's say his intentions are honourable. It doesn't change the fact that you didn't tell me about it. And I really want to know why.'

'Nick, please sit back down. I've apologized. I should have told you. What else can I say?'

'I don't know.'

'Look, he wants to meet me for lunch tomorrow. Why don't you come with me and then you can hear for yourself what he has to say.'

And then the awkwardness would be halved and she wouldn't have to worry about keeping secrets.

'So, you're meeting him again. Well, I suppose I should be grateful you've mentioned it.'

'Now you're just being pathetic. And I really don't see why all this is so important.' She began to pack away the Chinese food. She'd deserved the dressing down for keeping her meeting with Jonathan from him, but how long was she going to have to pay for it?

'Well, it was obviously important enough for you to hide it from me.'

'For God's sake! I didn't hide it from you. If I was really hiding it from you I wouldn't be telling you now. Do you know something? Perhaps I didn't tell you because I knew you'd react like this.'

'What d'you mean?'

'I knew you'd be jealous.'

That's what all this was about. If this had been about anyone else offering the money, other than the boy she'd pledged to marry years ago, they wouldn't even be having this conversation.

'I'm not jealous.'

'Well, you're doing a pretty good impression of someone who is.'

'And if I remember correctly, you made lying to people a full-time occupation not so long ago.'

The comment was well below the belt and she felt her temper erupt and take over. She slapped him, hard across the face and then stepped back in shock at what she'd done.

He took in a sharp breath and just looked back at her, unmoving.

She pushed past him, ran out of the gazebo and raced off up the road.

Thirteen

She caught her breath and put a hand to her chest. The blood was pumping so hard she could hear it echoing in her ears. She pushed open the door of Casey's diner.

Blond-haired Casey was wiping down the surfaces and removing some doughnuts from display when Freya arrived at the counter.

'Hey, Freya, no doctor's outfit tonight,' Casey asked, smiling.

'No and I can see you're missing a gorilla suit. Can I have a large cup of tea and a blueberry muffin?'

'Doughnuts are two for one. It's that time of night,' he offered, indicating the remaining doughnuts on display.

'I'll take four and some chocolate sauce.'

'I'll bring it over.'

She went across the room and sat down at her favourite table in the corner by the jukebox. Billy Ray Cyrus was playing. Inappropriate honky tonk that didn't suit her mood.

The bell above the diner door rang and she raised her head. Nicholas entered and she hurriedly put her head back down and pretended to be engrossed in the menu.

'Hey, Nick. How you doing?' Casey asked as he appeared from the kitchen and came back to the counter.

'I'm fine, Casey thanks. Could I get a coffee? Strong black?'

'Sure, I'll bring it over.'

He walked over to Freya's table and stood in front of her. His presence made her look up.

'Is this seat taken?' he asked, indicating the chair opposite her.

'Yes.'

'Well I don't see anyone sitting there and I have Chinese food.' He shook the bag at her.

'I'm expecting someone. I've just called Jonny and told him to come right over and have his way with me on this very table.'

He sat down opposite her, reached out and took her hands in his.

'I'm sorry.' His tone was soft.

'Sorry for what?'

'For what I said and for being stupid. You were right. I was jealous.'

'I'm sorry I hit you.'

'I'm sorry I provoked you. I should know by now you have a mean right hook.'

'I'm sorry I didn't tell you about Jonny the minute he walked into the office.'

'I think I overreacted because of who it was. He was the only man you trusted to tell everything to before you met me. He was important to you, you loved him.'

'I loved him when I was seventeen. I don't love him now. Anyway, you have to trust me.'

She looked across at him. Her handsome fiancé, the man who graces magazine covers and wore swimwear on *David Letterman*.

'How bizarre is this conversation? *You're* the one idolised by millions of women, most of whom are a thousand times better looking than me. *You* snog a different actress every other month. If there's anyone who should be having a fit of jealousy here it's me.'

'One large tea, one coffee and four doughnuts with chocolate sauce.' Casey put the order on the table.

'You ordered doughnuts,' Nicholas remarked.

'I was depressed.'

'Can I share?'

'I suppose so. But no hogging the sauce.' She picked up a doughnut, tore some off and dipped it in the sauce.

'Listen, if Jonny's genuine about donating all that money and time to your project, I *do* think it's great,' Nicholas told her.

'Well I was suspicious of his intentions at first, but the trade off was I have to take some photographs of some of his hotels.'

'That doesn't sound like too bad a deal.'

'No and besides that, I really think he feels bad about the way he treated me. Everyone has a moment in their life when they take stock, think back, regret things and want to try and put them right. Perhaps this is his.'

'So, are we friends again?'

'Well that depends on how many doughnuts you're planning on eating.'

'I thought I might order a chilli burger with everything on it actually.'

'Make that two and we're BFFs.'

After food at Casey's, they got ice creams from the ice cream parlour and ate them on the walk back to their home. One of the joys of living in America was ice cream available all year round. Even though the night was almost as frosty as their dessert, it still tasted good.

'He has a crap car,' Freya said, her mouth full of ice cream.

'Who? Jonny? I thought you said he was a millionaire.'

'He is, but he obviously has bad taste in cars. And he had a driver.' She laughed at the absurdity.

'Then he obviously classed meeting you as an official function.'

'Either that or he's just plain lazy. Listen, I spoke to Emma today and told her we'd set a date for the wedding.'

'And can she make it?'

'Well, she actually came up with a different suggestion.'

'Oh?'

'She thought we might consider getting married in Corfu.'

'And what did you think about that idea?'

'What do *you* think?'

'I asked first.' He smiled.

'I quite like the idea. It's probably one of the only places in the world where we might actually get some privacy. We could stay with Emma and Yiannis at the villa and we could spend our honeymoon there, visiting all the places we didn't get to see together last time.'

'I think it sounds like a fantastic idea.'

'So shall we do it? The beach might be out, it's warmer than here but...'

'How about up at the fort? At sunset.'

'That sounds perfect.'

She touched his cheek with her hand and moved forward to kiss him.

'I love you,' she whispered.

'I love you too.'

He kissed her cheek then entered the security code for the front gate into the pad.

'Notice anything? No photographers,' he stated, leading the way through the gate as it swung open.

'We are going to be B-list celebrities before too much longer.'

'Well that wouldn't bother me. We would save a fortune on tea.'

As they approached the front porch Freya saw Willis sat by the door clawing savagely at something lying on the deck.

'Oh, Nick he's got a bird or something. Urgh, go and stop him.' She turned away and concentrating on finishing her ice cream.

'It's a crow. Hey, boy, get off it. Let me open the door and you can go inside,' he said to the cat, kicking the dead bird out of his reach.

'Is it dead?' Freya called.

'Yeah it's dead. Looks like it flew into the front door. The glass is smashed.'

Freya looked up at their front door and observed the jagged edges where the circular panel of glass had been.

'Looks like I'll have to call a glazier. I'm surprised it didn't set the alarm off. It must have hit quite hard,' Nicholas said, pushing open the door.

'Um, I think I might have forgotten to set the alarm when we left,' she admitted.

'Freya! You *must* set the alarm! Remember you promised. You said you'd cope with an alarm as long as we didn't have the electric fence or CCTV. You have to keep your end of the bargain.'

'I know, I know and I usually do. I just forgot. Blame Bruce and the lure of the spring rolls. Urgh! God,

Willis, don't rub your face against me it's got feathers and guts all over it.' She tried to evade the cat by hopping from one foot to the other.

'I'll call the window guys, see if they can come out tonight.' He headed into the kitchen.

'Ooo move the dead bird first please. I'm sure I read somewhere that crows are unlucky.'

'That one certainly was.'

Fourteen

'Do you think Matt and Susannah will still be able to make the wedding if we decide on Corfu?' Freya asked.

It was the following morning and they were sat at the dining table, eating for breakfast the Chinese they had started the night before.

'I'm sure they will and we can always pay for their flights.'

'I'm making a list of people to invite. I've got Matt and Susannah and little Jo obviously. Roger and Dionne, Emma, Yiannis and Melly, Mr and Mrs P. Then I'm kind of struggling.' She chewed the pen she was writing with. There was no one else she could think of unless she invited her ex-boyfriend Russell or people she'd met in jail.

'Well, you can add my Uncle Ted and my Aunt Carol. Though I don't expect they'll come because I haven't seen them since my parents' funeral. I ought to ask though.' He raised his head out of the script he was reading.

'So that's twelve. Do you think that's enough? I mean, I know we said we wanted a small wedding but ten people and two under fours?'

At this rate they wouldn't need catering, they could just ask Samos to open the kebab shop and serve everyone *gyros*.

'We only need two witnesses, so ten is good. And probably just enough for a game of beach volleyball after the ceremony,' he joked.

'I keep telling you it isn't that warm there in December. There might be snow. Are you reading through that same script?' She put her pen down and jabbed at a sweet and sour ball with her fork.

'Yeah, I'm still not sure about it. It's not a role that's going to stretch me.'

'So don't do it. What's the point of doing something if you aren't going to get anything out of it?'

'They've offered me fifteen million.'

'Shit! Fifteen million! That could…'

'Go towards building another hospital. Or buying more equipment. Or helping set up another Every Day centre.'

He'd read her mind. Fifteen million for one movie was extortionate but how much good could that do for so many other people?

'But, Nick, regardless of the money, don't do it if it isn't right for you.'

'I don't know. It's a whole lot of money for not a lot of work.' He sighed.

'Money isn't everything. No matter how wisely you spend it, or give it away.'

'No, I know. Hey, why don't you read the script, see what you think.' He pushed the wad of paperwork over to her.

'Me? Oh, I don't know. You know I'm not really one for reading.'

She got bored halfway through a postcard.

'No, but you *are* one for films. I'd value your opinion.'

'Well OK, I'll give it a go.' The intercom buzzed and Freya jumped up. 'Ooo that's Amos with the post.'

'Are you expecting something important because you leapt up like your life depended on it.'

'Not my life, our wedding. I called Sharona Owen yesterday afternoon and asked her to send me some wedding dress catalogues.'

Sharona Owen was a well-known designer and one of her specialties was plus-size gowns.

'Sadie Fox not getting your business then?'

'Sadie Fox would never be able to get hold of enough material to dress me. She's used to dressing models with stomachs as flat as ironing boards and personalities to match. Hello!' Freya greeted, pressing the button to speak into the intercom.

'Hello, Freya this is Brian. Are you receiving me? Over.'

'Brian? What are you doing here? I thought you were Amos.'

'Today I *am* Amos. Over. I have the mail. Repeat. I have the mail. Over.'

'Oh, OK. I'm buzzing you in. Come up to the house. Over.' She pressed the button to open the front gate.

'Brian?' Nicholas questioned, putting the breakfast plates on the countertop.

'Yes and he has the mail. Over.' She headed to the front door.

She opened it up and Brian, dressed in a postman's uniform, hurried up the driveway towards the house.

'Good morning, Nick. Good morning, Freya. Over.' Brian walked up the steps and onto the front porch.

'You don't have to say *over* now, Brian. We're not on the intercom, we're right here,' Freya said, smiling.

'Sorry. Right, here is your mail.' He dug into the sack across his shoulder and pulled out two large packets and two smaller letters.

'Gimme! Gimme!" Freya ordered. She snatched the large packets from Brian's hands and ran back into the house.

'One of those was for you,' Brian informed Nicholas, handing him the smaller letters.

'Thanks, Brian. Freya's a little over excited about wedding dresses.'

'I heard about that. Tell me, is her father really dead?' He adjusted his hat.

'Sorry?'

'It's on the front page of *The Gazette* this morning. Here, I've got a copy with me, and I'm sure I heard something about it on the news too. Although, I *was* eating at the time and my hearing's not quite as good when I'm eating as it is when I'm not.' He produced the newspaper from the mail sack.

Nicholas took hold of the paper and read the headline. 'Freya Fuels Father Feud'. He looked at the photograph. It was one of the publicity shots from their hospital visit the previous day.

'Brian, can I keep this?' Nicholas asked him, folding the paper up.

'It was seventy five cents.'

'I'll shout you a meal at Casey's the next time you're there.'

'Three courses? With drinks and sides?'

'Whatever you want. I promise.'

'Sure, keep the paper.'

She licked her lips as she looked at the dresses in the catalogue. She'd bypassed the frills and the lace and was gazing at heavenly creations she might be able to get a dual use from. Some of Nicholas' film parties needed glamour. She heard him come back into the room.

'Don't come any closer. I've seen a couple of frocks I like and I do not want you getting even a peek at any of them.' She picked up the brochure and held it against her chest.

'You might want to look at this.' He put the newspaper down in front of her.

She looked at the headline and then read out loud.

'Nicholas Kaden and fiancée Freya Johnson, visited Carlton General Hospital yesterday to unveil the facility's new scanning equipment paid for by the Nicholas Kaden Foundation. During the visit they met with patients of the cancer ward, most of whom have limited life expectancy. One such young patient, who cannot be named, was heard asking Miss Johnson about her upcoming nuptials and in particular whether her father, billionaire business tycoon Eric Lawson-Peck, would be attending the ceremony. A source claims Miss Johnson seemed particularly uncomfortable when asked about her father and ultimately informed the patient her father was dead. Eric Lawson-Peck, alive and well, attended a reception in New York last night where he refused to comment. Last year, Freya Johnson's ex-partner, Russell Buchanan, claimed Miss Johnson had been abused by her father throughout her childhood and made countless accusations of improper conduct relating to both his personal and business life. These claims were strongly refuted by Lawson-Peck and Miss Johnson issued an apology. Shit!'

'Good, huh?'

'I don't understand. How the hell did they get hold of this? I mean, they've misquoted me to start with. I didn't actually say it like that and I didn't blurt it across the ward. I said it to Katherine and you were the only one there. She's a kid and from the look of her yesterday she was in no state to give interviews to *The Gazette*,' Freya exclaimed.

This was bad. Anything with her father involved was bad but this, telling the world he was dead! Nothing good was going to come out of that. How stupid was she? Why had she said it? She didn't think. That had always been her trouble and now she was neck deep in just that.

'Well, I don't know how they got hold of it but they did and they printed it. Brian also said he heard something about it on the news this morning.'

'Oh my God. What am I going to do?' She put her hand to her chest as the breath caught there.

'Look, calm down. Let's think rationally about this.'

'Think rationally?! How can I think rationally? My father's going to take one look at this and think I wanted it. The paper's already asked him about it and he refused to comment. What does that say?'

'It says he knows how to handle the media and he'll let his press agent take care of it.'

'Oh no, no. You don't know my father like I do. He won't be letting anyone else handle this. He'll be handling it himself. If there's one thing I know about my father, it's that he doesn't mind getting his hands dirty.'

'Freya, calm down. What d'you think's going to happen?'

'What's going to happen is what always happens. He's going to punish me.' She felt the tears brimming in her eyes.

'That isn't going to happen. Come here, come on.' He pulled her into his arms. 'It's not so bad. I mean you said he was dead. It was an off-the-cuff remark. It didn't mean anything.'

His words did nothing to comfort her. She knew the man. She knew how he operated.

'He won't like it. It won't be acceptable, for me to speak out like that, off-the-cuff remark or not. I've put him in the papers and brought everything all back up again. He's going to do something about it, Nick. He's going to hurt you or me, or Emma. Oh God! What if he hurts Melly?' Her voice came out as a shriek and the tears fell.

'Listen, that isn't going to happen. I mean, read the article again. It's just rubbish. So, someone overheard you say your father's dead? What's that really going to mean to him? You aren't part of his life anymore. To you he *is* dead,' he reminded.

'He just won't like it, Nick. He'll feel insulted and people will be looking at him wondering why he isn't going to his only child's wedding. Then the rumours will start and people will start asking questions again about all the things Russell told *Shooting Stars* magazine,' Freya told him.

'The truth, you mean.'

'Yes, the truth. But dealing the truth was too much of a price to pay and it was over. But now? God, why can't I keep my big mouth shut?' She wiped at her eyes, then put her fingers in her mouth to chew the nails.

'Come on, babe, it's going to be fine. Look, if you're really worried let *me* sort it out. I'll get Sandra on to it. We'll issue a statement telling everyone you were misquoted and we'll cut this off before it has a chance to do any damage, to us or your father,' he said, running a hand through Freya's hair.

'It's too late, it's done and he won't let it go again.' Her voice was trembling now. That's what that man did to her, terrified her. All the happiness and excitement she felt earlier about her wedding and choosing a dress had all but evaporated.

The phone rang.

'That'll be the start of it. That will be a reporter,' Freya stated, letting go of Nicholas and going back over to the newspaper.

'No it won't. Hello,' he greeted.

Freya looked again at the photograph on the front page of the paper and racked her brain as to who would have overheard her comment about her father.

'Yeah she's here. No, that's OK, I'll just pass you over.' He held the handset out. 'It's Sasha.'

She took the phone and he put a strong arm around her, kissing her cheek.

'Listen, I'm going to grab a shower. Don't worry about it, OK? I'll deal with it, I promise.' He squeezed her free hand. 'Oh and these letters are for you too. One of them looks like it's from a shopping channel.' He passed her the rest of her mail and left the kitchen.

She put the phone to her ear and raised her shoulder to keep it in place as she opened the first letter.

'Hello, Sasha. Is the office on fire?'

'No. Sorry to call you at home again but I've had journalists calling already this morning asking about your father. I just wondered what, if anything, you wanted me to say.'

'Nothing, Sasha, just say nothing. I know that's something *I* usually can't manage but I'm sure you're far more adept at it.' She let out a sigh and took the letter from the envelope.

'You don't sound surprised they've been calling. Has something happened? Is everything OK?'

'I'm headline news again. That's what's happened. Good photograph but terrible article.' She looked at the letter in her hands and couldn't stop herself from reacting. 'Oh my God!'

'Freya? Are you OK?'

Freya stared at the letter. There was one word stuck onto the piece of paper, made out of newspaper cuttings.

Bitch

Freya stared at the word, then turned the piece of paper over to look at the reverse side. It was blank.

'Freya? Are you still there?'

'Sorry, Sasha, I'm still here.' She folded up the paper and slipped it into the pocket of her robe.

'So, what shall I tell the journalists?'

'Nothing. Say I have no comment to make. Listen, I probably won't be in this morning. What's in the diary?' She picked up *The Gazette*.

'Diana Farrington at ten. Miles Blake at eleven thirty and Jonathan Sanders at one.'

'Right, well postpone Diana. Do you think you could see Miles? I'll make it for one.'

'No problem. Freya, are you sure everything's OK?'

'I'm fine, honestly. I'll see you later.'

She ended the call and put the phone down on the countertop. One shaky breath later and she felt like passing out. It was starting all over again.

Fifteen

'I don't want to wait.'

It was almost one and she was travelling to Carlton with Nicholas. That morning, after the news about her father and the hate mail, she had walked into Mayleaf, bought a hair colour and spent the rest of the time dying it dark brown.

'Jeez! Will you look at this traffic? What is going on?' He pulled into the queue of cars waiting to go the same way.

'Nick, I don't want to wait to get married.' She put her hand on his leg, trying to get his attention.

'What d'you mean?" He turned to look at her.

'Twenty second of December, it's too far away. I don't want to wait that long.'

'Are you kidding me? It's next month!'

'I know, but it's the *end* of next month and what's the point of waiting? I mean we love each other, right? And we don't need anyone else there really. And if we just went off and did it without telling anyone then the press wouldn't be hassling us and we'd have the quiet wedding we want.' The words flew out of her mouth at top speed.

'But yesterday you really wanted to get married on Corfu. You were excited about that and I don't believe you really want to have your special day without Emma there.'

'I just want to marry you and you said it didn't matter how we did it. You said it was the commitment that's important and I agree.'

'This is just a reaction to the newspaper article. Freya, I know it's got to you and I understand why, but it *will* be alright, you know. Primarily, your father is a businessman and I really don't believe he would let a news feature, as pathetic and pointless as that one, stir him up.'

'It isn't anything to do with the article. It really isn't. I love you, Nick. I just want to get married. Don't you want to do it? We could just go off somewhere and get married and spend our honeymoon driving round the country on the Harley. We could stay at cheap motels, drink beer and eat junk food,' she suggested.

It was sounding good and she had kept the desperation out of her voice.

'We can still spend our honeymoon doing that if that's what you want.'

'Why don't we just get a flight to Vegas on Friday night and just do it?'

'Because I don't believe that's what you want. What about the dress you were planning?'

'I've got plenty of dresses. Well, maybe one or two.'

'Freya, come on, this isn't right. I want our wedding day to be something we remember for years and years to come. I like the idea of going back to Corfu.'

'Yes, me too. I really did. But do you know what? The weather forecast is horrendous. They're talking snow and thunder storms. The works.'

'I don't believe you.'

She let out a sigh and turned to look out of the passenger window.

'December twenty second isn't that far away you know. Why don't I make some calls today and see if I can arrange a few things. Maybe you could speak to Emma and let her know we'll be seeing her soon.'

'Yeah, OK.'

There was no enthusiasm in her voice at all. Everything felt bleak now that newspaper article was in the public domain.

'Look, I promised I would sort things out with the newspaper and your father. Trust me, Freya, I won't let him hurt you again.'

'It isn't *me* I'm worried about.'

'Well, I can look after myself and I have Roger. But if it's Emma you're worried about, I can arrange someone to be with her and Yiannis. But I really think it's jumping the gun. Besides, if we really thought your father was going to start hurting people, I'd want to be talking to the police about it.'

'Could you arrange it so she wouldn't know?'

'Freya, are you serious about this? You really think your father would try to hurt Emma?'

'Yes, I keep telling you. You have no idea what he's capable of.'

'I just think that, given the situation between you, he can't really make an issue about you telling someone he isn't coming to our wedding,' Nicholas said.

'Perhaps I should invite him.'

That thought made her more alert. That might be a way to get out of all this. She would contact him. She would invite him to the wedding. He might not come. If he did come, she wouldn't have to spend any time with him. And then it would be over. Her duty would be done and public opinion would be settled.

'What?! That wasn't a serious comment was it?'

'Well, it would be a sure fire way to settle things down. It would make the media think there was no feud and whoever sold this story to *The Gazette* wasn't a credible source. In that case, maybe we should have a huge wedding and get as much publicity as possible.'

'Freya! Stop this right now. For one, that isn't the wedding we want and secondly, if you think I'm going to have your father at our wedding, then maybe you're marrying the wrong man.' He focused back on the traffic.

'I don't want him at our wedding and for what it's worth I wish he really *was* dead. But I'm just trying to think of ways to stop this in its tracks. Because you know what the press are like. They will pick and dig and ferret around and they won't stop.'

The tears were there again. Filling up her eyes, giving her clouded vision.

'Freya, you have to trust me. I will sort this out. But until I do, would you really like me to get someone to keep an eye on Emma and Yiannis?'

'Yes, I really would.'

'Then I'll arrange it. I'll get someone over there today and I'll make sure all the security systems at the villa are checked. OK?' he asked her.

She nodded.

'Now, I don't want you worrying anymore about that damn newspaper article. What I do want you worrying about is wedding dresses, invitations and catering in Corfu.'

She nodded again and smiled, wiping her eyes with her hands.

'By the way,' he said pulling the car away as traffic began to move. 'I love your hair that colour.'

Sixteen

When they arrived at Exposure there was a hoard of photographers outside the gate. They started to shout and take pictures as soon as they set eyes on the Ferrari. Once through the gates and inside the car park, Freya noticed Jonathan's car was already there.

'Well, I suppose the press pack would be here. I expect I'm all over CNN.' She let out a heavy sigh.

'Just ignore them or say *no comment*. There isn't much they can do with that.'

'Apart from thinking I'm a moody cow.'

'Which they should already know by now.'

'Hey!' She hit his arm playfully.

'Listen, I've got to go. I'm late for my meeting and you know what Sandra's like about schedules.'

'Sure, you go. Pick me up about five?'

'Five it is. Hey, do you fancy going downtown tonight? Playing a little roulette? Visiting a few bars?'

'Stopping at the all-you-can-eat for twenty dollars restaurant?'

'Naturally.'

'That sounds great. Oh bugger, where's my handbag?' She looked around the footwell.

'Did you have it when you left home?'

'I don't know, maybe not. I was in such a hurry I probably left it there. Don't worry, it just has my mobile in it and I'm sure I can do without that for a day. Well perhaps not, but I'll deal with it. You go, I don't want to make you later than you already are.'

As she went to step out of the car, Jonathan appeared at the entrance to the office and came out to greet her.

'Hi. New hair colour. I like it. Here, let me help you.' He took her hand and helped her get out of the low car.

'I'm fine, thanks.'

There was that awkward feeling again in the pit of her stomach.

Jonathan bent to look in through the open door of the car and he leveled a smile at Nicholas.

'I heard the car pull up. She's a beauty. It's Nicholas isn't it? Hi there, I'm Jonathan. It's a real pleasure to meet you,' he said, holding out his hand.

'Actually I prefer Nick. I've heard a lot about you.' They shook hands.

'What have you been telling him, Freya? No stories about me terrorising the neighbourhood in my teens I hope.' He laughed.

'Well I...'

This was truly weird and she couldn't wait for it to be over.

'Freya tells me you want to make a big investment into her Every Day project,' Nicholas continued.

'Yes I do. I have to admit I'm not usually one for charity work, but coming from a reasonably poor background myself, I thought Freya's vision for the needy was inspired.'

'You'd better go, Nick. You don't want to be late for your meeting.'

If she thought pushing the Ferrari would help she'd be doing it.

'I'm sorry, I'm holding you up. Please, don't stay on my account.' He stepped back from the car.

'I hope it goes OK. Give me a call later,' she urged, leaning into the car for a little privacy.

'I will. I'll see you.' He kissed her lips.

'It was nice to meet you, Nick. Maybe we could get together some time, have a drink,' Jonathan called.

'Yeah, sure.' Nicholas pulled up the windows and drove towards the exit.

'That is a great car. I have one myself of course, but not that particular model. And mine's yellow. I was told the red version was just a little too *Magnum*.' He followed the car with his eyes as Nicholas left through the gate.

'I'm sorry I'm late, I've had a bit of a hectic morning. Can I just check in with Sasha before we go to lunch?' Freya asked moving towards the door of the building.

'Of course. Shall I wait in the car?'

'Do you still have the driver?'

'Yes I do.'

'Then you'd better go and keep him company. I won't be long.'

She pushed open the door and entered the reception area. The part-time secretary was behind the desk.

'Hey, Avril. Where's Sasha?'

'Hello, Miss Johnson. Sasha had to go out on an appointment so she asked me to come in a little early. I didn't mind.'

'Oh OK. Well, make sure I pay you for the extra time, won't you? Keep reminding me, Avril. Write it on a

Post It and stick it to a patisserie bag if you have to.' She leafed through her appointment book.

'I will. Patisserie bag, noted.'

'Right, well, I'm going on a lunch appointment with Mr Sanders. I should be back by three but I don't have my mobile with me so you won't be able to contact me. I assume Sasha has briefed you about the journalists.' She backed towards the door.

'Yes she has, we are making no comment. Miss Johnson?' Avril called before Freya could exit.

'Yes, Avril.'

'I do like your hair that colour. It makes you look very mature.'

'Mature? *Mature* as in old? Oh my God, does it?' She scrutinised her reflection in the glass panels of the door.

'Perhaps that was the wrong word.'

'Perhaps I was too hasty saying I would pay you over time.'

She left the building and made her way over to Jonathan's car. She opened the back door.

'Do I look old?' she asked him.

'Hmm, you'll have to get a little closer for me to tell. I can't quite get a good enough look at the bags under your eyes from this angle.'

'God, it's useless asking you. Where are we going for lunch?'

'Where d'you want to go?'

'Can we just get a hot dog or something? I really don't feel like a restaurant.'

'Of course. Ken, take us to the best hot dog vendor around here.' Jonathan called to the driver.

'I promise I won't get chilli sauce on your seats.'

'Who said I was going to let you eat in the car.'

Twenty minutes later Ken stopped the car in a pull-in just across the road from a fun fair.

'The guy who runs the hot dog stand at this fair has been cooking dogs for over thirty years,' Ken told them.

'Well, Ken I would say that constitutes being the best hot dog vendor around here. So shall we go and see what thirty years on the job has taught him?' Jonathan asked Freya.

'You want us to go to the fair? Have you felt how cold it is out there?!' She looked out the window at the amusements.

'Well, I could see if the hot dog man delivers or send Ken over there, but wouldn't it be more fun to go ourselves? I'll give you my coat,' he offered.

'No, that's OK. I have triple layers.'

'Come on, Freya, you used to love the fair,' he reminded. He opened the car door.

'When I was young, unlined and unbagged and had decent hair.' She stepped out and the ice cold wind hit her straight away. She buttoned her coat up all the way and wished she had a hat.

They entered the fair, found Max's Hot Dogs and bought two large sausages in rolls with onions and chilli sauce.

'Ferris wheel?' Jonathan suggested biting into his food.

'While we're eating?' Chilli sauce drizzled down her chin.

'Why not?'

'Well, from what I can remember about going to the fair with you, you used to throw up on the Ferris wheel.' She let out a laugh.

'That was a story made up by Carl Curtis because he was jealous I had a girlfriend and he didn't. He liked Emma remember, but she wasn't interested. You and I went on the big wheel several times together. I remember a lot of things about that ride but throwing up isn't one of them.'

Freya felt her cheeks redden and she hid her face by taking a huge bite of sausage and almost burning her lips.

'Come on, let's have a ride on it. Or are you too grown up and old to enjoy the simple pleasures in life?'

'No, I'm not too old and I'm not going to puke either. I'm the girl who ate a four course meal and half a dozen puddings on a cross channel ferry in a force seven storm. I have no idea what motion sickness is.'

'I'm arranging some plans to be drawn up of the site at Gatebrook to show how I envisage the development.'

They were high above the park now, swinging in the air as they slowly rotated around the wheel.

'Good, well I can show you what we have planned for Chesterville and we can coordinate the two.'

'I saw *The Gazette* today,' Jonathan stated.

'Oh, you did. You and the entire country. I've had journalists phoning the studio all morning apparently and all because I made one stupid, but private, remark.'

'I know it isn't any of my business and you can tell me to shut up if you like. But don't you think this awkwardness with Eric's been going on too long now?' He looked across at Freya.

'*Awkwardness*?' Freya said, looking straight back at Jonathan.

'Well, you said one of the main reasons you fell out with him was because you thought he'd parted us deliberately. Now I've told you that wasn't the case. Perhaps your getting married is the perfect time to lay matters to rest.'

'Did you get me up on this Ferris wheel to talk about this because you knew the only way out was down?'

'One of my weak points is family. I don't like to see families torn apart just because no one will budge an inch on anything. I mean, you could both hold your hands up and say *OK I've made mistakes* and then you could move on, start afresh.'

'If I wanted to feel like I was appearing on *Oprah* I could probably get an audience with the woman herself.'

'I am sure Eric doesn't like the situation any more than you do. Who would want to be estranged from their daughter?'

'Look, can we stick to talking about the project please? There was more to it than being pissed with him for making you leave town, believe me.'

'Sometimes, in business, you have to do things you aren't proud of to get what you want.'

'What exactly are you saying? That the things he did were justified?'

'Obviously I can't comment on anything specific he did back then. But speaking as a business man, I know what a cut throat place the business world can be. I know what risks you have to take.'

'Well, Jonny, it was never about what he did to make his billions. It was how he behaved when he walked back through the front door of the house every night. It was how I'd hide in my wardrobe if he was in a black mood. It was about him telling me over and over again how he wanted a son and what a disappointment I was. And it was about him stabbing me in the arm with a bread knife.' She pulled at the collar of her jumper and revealed her shoulder. There was a small but deep scar at the top of her arm.

'You always said that scar was where you scraped it on a nail,' Jonathan remarked. He swallowed.

'I did, didn't I? Now I wonder who made up that story?'

She was shaking now. Not because the wind was twice as cold up high in the sky, but because she'd been forced to remember those times again. Her childhood with that monster.

'My God.' He put his hands to his mouth.

'So you see, you may have this happy family ideal in your head, but it is never going to happen in my world.' She straightened the collar of her jumper.

'I didn't think the article was true. I was sure Russell Buchanan was cashing in on you and embellishing things.'

'You read that article about me?'

'It was all over the papers.'

'But you didn't believe it? Why not? I told you what my parents were like.'

'I don't know. I just didn't think anyone could really do those things to their child.'

'You don't know my father. He'll stop at nothing to get what he wants and that article in the paper today has probably just made my life hell again.'

'You think Eric will be displeased?'

'It's been reported in the national press that his only child's told someone he isn't coming to her wedding. Then she topped it off by saying he was dead. That translates to *she wishes he was dead*. Wouldn't you be displeased? He'll be furious.'

'What do you think he'll do?'

'You want me to be honest?'

'Yes.'
'I think he'll probably try to kill me.'

Seventeen

That night Nicholas and Freya went into the pandemonium that was central Hollywood. Nicholas had lived there before they'd moved to Mayleaf. It was like being in an all-action entertainment park. Great for a night out but not so pleasant to live in.

They'd visited three bars already and had been tailed by paparazzi the whole time. Now, they'd decided on a members-only casino, just to get a break from being photographed.

'So are we agreed? We gamble a hundred thousand dollars and that's it. And whatever we make we split between my charity and yours,' Nicholas said.

'Make it a hundred thousand dollars each. I feel lucky.' She smiled.

'OK.' He put his arm around her and they headed to the cashier.

'Mr Kaden, Miss Johnson, it's nice to see you again,' Sammy, the middle-aged croupier at the roulette table greeted as they sat down.

'Hi, Sammy. How's the wheel going tonight? Anyone win big?' Freya asked.

'As you know, I'm not allowed to provide you with that information. Let's just say I think Lady Luck is wearing red tonight.'

'Our chips are just being brought down from upstairs. We'll eat the nuts while we wait,' Freya told him, scooping up a handful.

'So, how did your lunch with Jonny go?'

'Fine. He's having some plans drawn up for me to look at. Then his architect can get together with mine and fight it out.'

'He wasn't what I expected,' Nicholas admitted.

'No? Well, what were you expecting?'

'I didn't think he would be so confident.'

'Oh he's always been like that.'

'I'm not sure I liked it.'

'He's a talker that's all and he's developed a plummy accent. Sometimes that comes across as arrogance. I don't think it's really that.'

'Well you're the one who knows him.'

'I really think he means well with the charity and I can't turn down that sort of help.' Her phone rang and she took it out and checked the screen. 'It's Emma, I'd better answer it. Look, I won't be a minute, stick twenty thousand dollars on red number twenty.'

She got off her seat and headed out of the room towards the toilets.

'Hi, Em.'

'Hi. I just thought I'd give you a Melly update.'

'Oh how is she? You sound better. Has she perked up a bit?'

'She's almost fully recovered. She's keeping down her milk and she's been really happy so far today. We got a good night's sleep last night.'

'That's great news. I'm so pleased.'

'So, how are things with you?'

'Oh you know, hovering between chaotic and terrifying. I'm putting a brave face on things.'

The whole of the sentence sounded less than convincing.

'What's happened?'

Freya explained about the newspaper article.

'I don't know what to say. This is the last thing you need when you're planning to get married next month,' Emma told her.

'I know and we've thought about it and we'd really like to get married on Corfu. But after all this I don't know whether it's going to be possible.'

She could almost feel the perfect wedding dream evaporating.

'I don't think you should let this newspaper article dictate where you get married.'

'It isn't that. It's what my father might decide to do about it.'

'What does Nick say?'

'He tells me not to worry about it. He says my father won't be concerned and everything will be happy ever after and roses around the door. But I keep telling him he doesn't know my father like I do. And…there's something I haven't told Nick yet.' She dropped her voice to a whisper.

'What?'

'I got a letter this morning, in the post. It had the word "bitch" on it. It was like one of those ransom notes you get in movies. All the letters were cut up out of a newspaper.'

'Oh my God!'

'It's my father and that's just the start.'

'Freya, why haven't you told Nick?'

'Because I want to try and handle this myself.'

'Freya, I really think you should tell Nick.'

'I *will* tell him, just not yet.'

'Well, if you're sure you know what you're doing.'

'Yeah I do. Listen, I'm going to have to go because I've left Nick at the roulette wheel with two hundred thousand dollars in chips coming and I've told you what he's like at gambling.'

'You said he couldn't back a winner in a one horse race.'

'Exactly. I'll ring you tomorrow.'

'Oh, hang on, while you're on the phone…just tell Nick someone came round today to check the alarm system. It's all working fine.'

'Oh that's good. Yes, he said it was due to be checked. I'll tell him.'

Hearing that news made her slightly calmer about the situation. Emma, Yiannis and now Melly, were her family. They meant more to her than anything.

'OK, bye,' Emma ended.

Freya put her mobile back into her handbag and took the chance to look at herself in the mirror. Seeing herself with brown hair surprised her for a second. She'd almost forgotten she'd dyed it. She pushed her hair behind her ears and adjusted her glasses. It was a different look and that was the main thing.

She left the ladies room and made her way back into the main room of the casino. Nicholas wasn't sat where she'd left him.

There were two new players, a man and a woman and Sammy was taking bets for the next spin.

'Hey, Sammy. Where did Nick go? Please don't tell me he lost everything already. I was only gone ten minutes.' She took a swig from her bottle of beer.

'He got a call from your driver and left. I think he tried to call you.'

'Oh.' She got back off her chair and walked towards the exit.

As she reached the door, Nicholas came back into the room. He had a serious expression on his face and straight away took Freya by the arm.

'We've got to go.' He urged her towards the door.

'What? What's going on?' He led her into the lobby.

'We've got to wait for the cops to get here.' He pressed a button for the elevator.

'Police? What for? What's happened? Why did Mikey call you?'

'The manager wants us to wait in his office.' He ran a hand through his hair.

'Nick, what's going on? For God's sake tell me.' The lift bell rang and the doors opened.

'Mikey's been taken to hospital. He was attacked.'

'What?! Oh my God! Is he going to be OK?' She put her hand to her mouth trying to take in what was being said.

'Freya, let's just get in the lift and get up to the manager's office.' He grabbed her hand.

'Is there more? Is there something you're not telling me?'

She wasn't sure she wanted to know. She felt sick.

'Let's get in the elevator. Please.' There was real concern in his tone.

'Nick, you're scaring me. Please tell me.'

Whatever it was she needed to hear it. She followed him into the lift and the doors closed.

'I don't exactly know what happened, but Mikey's been beat up pretty bad and the car is a mess. I mean a real mess. It looks like someone took an iron bar to it and just smashed it to pieces.'

Freya put her hands to her face and felt a surge of fear run through her. She began to feel like her chest was going to burst and the grip of terror rose up into her throat. Before she knew it she was struggling to breathe.

'Freya, come on, calm down. Take a deep breath. Slow breaths and look at me.' He took both of her hands and tried to turn her towards him.

'I...need to get...out of here.'

Her breathing was rapid now and she wasn't inhaling properly. Short, shallow bursts were all she could manage.

'It's three more floors, OK? Just keep taking deep breaths and look at me. Everything is going to be fine.'

Her chest was burning and she still couldn't get her breath. She felt out of control and dizzy.

The lift bell rang and the doors opened.

'We're here OK? Come on, let's get you sat down with a glass of water.'

'It's...my father...he's going to...' Freya tried to speak as Nicholas hurried them both along the corridor. Why was talking difficult? It came so naturally to her. Now it was exhausting.

'Don't try to speak, just breathe.'

She leaned into him for support.

'I...' she began.

She felt really lightheaded now. As if she'd sucked in the gas from a helium balloon. Walking wasn't so easy. In fact lying down seemed really appealing. She slumped to the floor.

'Freya? Oh God! Martin! Call an ambulance!' Nicholas yelled.

Eighteen

Freya opened her eyes and immediately shut them again. There was a bright white light positioned directly over her head. It could only mean one thing. She was in hospital where nice subtle lighting didn't exist. She felt sick and her mouth was dry.

'Freya,' Nicholas whispered.

She felt his fingers running softly through her hair and she really wanted to go back to sleep.

'Freya, are you awake?'

She lifted her eyelids open again and this time turned her head slightly and looked at Nicholas. He was sat in the chair next to her, an anxious expression on his face. He took hold of her hand and brought it to his lips, kissing it.

'How's Mike?' Freya croaked. She tried to sit up but found she was attached to a drip and the tube tightened with every movement.

'He's going to be fine. Lie down, babe.'

'Is he still here?'

'He's going to be fine, Freya, honestly. Roger's here with him and he's called his wife. He has a couple of stitches and some bruising. The brain scan was clear.'

'Brain scan! He had a *brain* scan! Oh my God! I have to see him.' She tried sitting up again but her head span the second she accelerated her movements past snail pace.

'Freya, please try and stay calm. The doctor says you've got to rest.'

'Well the doctor doesn't know me very well does he? You know how much I hate hospitals and what I hate more than hospitals is laying still. Can we go home? Where's my handbag?' She scanned the room for signs of familiarity and started to peel away the tape holding the drip in position.

'Freya, come on, don't make this difficult. The doctor says you're dehydrated and you passed out.'

'I left my bag at the casino. It has my phone in and my purse and…' she started.

'Don't worry about the damn bag. I'll call Martin, the manager and have him find it. Freya, you got so worked up you fainted.'

He was repeating himself. Not because he thought she hadn't heard the first time, but to hammer the point home. She'd got worked up over her father and what he had arranged for Mike and she'd blacked out. It wasn't like that had never happened before.

'I know what I did but I'm fine now. I just want to go home.' She finally managed to sit up.

'Look, stay in bed, just for a minute. I'll go and tell the doctor you're awake and see what I can do. Here, have some water.' He passed her a plastic cup.

She took a sip of the cool liquid and watched Nicholas leave the room. She took a deep breath and put her hand to her chest. It still felt tight and her head was woolly. She remembered the last time this had happened. She'd been on a flight from Athens to London having ended her relationship with Nicholas and having just spoken to her father. He was the cause of it. Like he was the cause of everything ugly that happened in her life.

Nicholas came back into the room followed by a tall, white-haired, doctor. He had a moustache and a smile. His name badge introduced him as Dr. Mark Stone.

'Hello, Freya. I'm glad you're awake. My name is…' the doctor began. He sat on the edge of Freya's bed.

'Dr. Mark Stone, so I see. Why's that name familiar to me?'

'Ah well, you're most probably thinking of Dr. Mark Sloane. Some of my patients say it isn't just my name that connects me. Do you think I bear a little resemblance to Dick Van Dyke?' He straightened himself up and pushed his glasses down his nose.

'*Diagnosis Murder*! Of course!'

'I'm afraid Freya's a bit of a TV addict, Doc.' Nicholas informed.

'Well for that I have no cure. Say, Nick, could you get Freya another cup of water while I talk privately with her for a moment?' Dr. Stone suggested.

'Sure,' he agreed. He gave Freya's hand a reassuring squeeze.

'It's OK, Dr. Stone. Anything you have to tell me, you can say in front of Nick.'

They'd promised no more secrets and, if she was honest, she didn't want to know something she might feel she had to keep from him. She was good at doing that just lately.

'Humour an old doctor will you, Freya? At my age I do tend to like my routines.' The doctor smiled at her.

'It's OK, babe. I'll just be outside and you can fill me in on what the doc says later.'

'I have to admit I really just want to be alone with a pretty young lady. I have to take my chances when they present themselves.' Dr. Stone let out a laugh as Nicholas left the room.

Freya propped herself up in the bed and looked straight at the doctor.

'Look, Dr. Stone, can I go home now? I know what happened to me. My blood pressure went through the roof and I passed out. You gave me some vile sedative which is why I feel like crap and my throat feels like I've swallowed a whole bag of rock hard pork scratchings.' She threw the sheet off her legs.

'Pork what?' Dr. Stone queried.

'Never mind. Just go and get me whatever form I need to sign to get myself out of here.'

'Freya, have you had an episode like this before?'

'Yes, and the very last time a doctor tried to keep me in hospital against my will he ended up getting admitted himself.' She tried to shuffle herself off the bed.

'Freya, please hear me out. I know Nick's very worried about you.' He put a hand on her arm.

She sat still on the bed and let out a sigh, avoiding the doctor's gaze.

'Have you had any episodes like this before?' he asked again.

'A few,' she admitted.

'How long ago was the last one?' He started making notes on his clipboard.

'It was about eight or nine months ago. But before that I hadn't had an attack for over ten years.'

'And before that - ten or so years ago - did you have random attacks or was there a frequency or pattern to things?'

'Are you sure you're an MD and not a shrink?'

She was finding the questioning uncomfortable. She didn't like thinking about ten years ago or any time before that.

'Is there anything you'd like to tell me, Freya? Perhaps there's a trigger to the attacks?'

'I had an unsatisfactory parental role model. That seemed to affect the frequency.'

'I see and was that a contributing factor to tonight's attack do you think?'

'Our driver, our friend, was attacked and our car was wrecked. I think it had more to do with that.'

'OK, I'm just trying to get a little background on your condition that's all. Well, we did give you a sedative, Freya. But I have to tell you your attack tonight was extremely serious. Your body actually went into shock and shock at its most acute form can cause death.'

'Like too much alcohol, cigarettes and fried food?'

'Much more deadly and faster acting that any of those. I think your condition is something we should start to monitor carefully.'

'My *condition*?! Oh, Dr. Stone, I don't have a *condition*. It's a blood pressure and a mild anxiety thing. And like I said I haven't had an attack for years. I even went through the deep-breathing-blowing-into-a-paper-bag course. I'm fine, honestly.'

'Freya, it was lucky Nick got you here so quickly or we might not be having this conversation now.'

'I don't want tranquilisers or valium or any other pills that are going to turn me into a head case,' Freya stated.

'That's fine, I wasn't planning on prescribing anything at present. And that leads me on to the next issue.'

'The next issue?! Just how many issues do I have? I had nothing wrong with me an hour or so ago.'

'Well, when you were admitted we took some blood to run some precautionary tests. I just got the results back and...'

'I'm not my father's daughter? I have some rare type of DNA never been seen before?'

'All indicators flagged up you're pregnant.'

Freya felt her whole body stiffen. Her chest tightened and she clutched at the side of the bed. The head rush and dizziness were back.

'Here, come on. Lie down and take a breath.' The doctor steadied her and urged her backwards onto the pillow.

'There must be some mistake.'

She couldn't be pregnant. They weren't trying. They weren't married.

'Well, I can have the lab run the tests again if you'd like me to. But I have to say they were pretty conclusive. Until you told me about your history of attacks, I was thinking perhaps your changing hormone levels might have caused your collapse tonight.'

'I can't be pregnant, Dr. Stone. I'm thirty years old. I know all about contraception and how to use it. And I've been using it. I swear.'

'I don't doubt you have. As with anything in life, there's always an element of chance.'

'Look, there must be an error with the tests. Perhaps they've mixed up someone else's results with mine. It happens all the time, I've read about it. I mean one minute someone's told they're dying. The next minute some poor sod who was told they were fine's being buried. And the person who's been blowing everything, thinking he has only months to live is actually fitter than the proverbial butcher's dog. For God's sake can you take this drip out of my arm!' She tugged at the plastic tube.

'I'd prefer it if you left it in a little while longer until we have your fluids up. Not just for your sake, but for the baby.'

'I really can't be pregnant, Dr. Stone. So, please, get me a release form so I can go home.'

'I'd really like you to have a scan and then we can be a hundred per cent certain one way or the other.'

'No. No scans, no more tests and no more prodding and poking. Please, I just want to go home.'

Tears were in her eyes now and her breath was catching again. She wanted 'normal' back.

'OK, come on, take a deep breath. Here, dry your eyes. I'll go and get Nick.' He offered her a tissue from a box on the cabinet. She took one and wiped her eyes as the doctor left the room.

She couldn't be pregnant. She was careful. She'd always been careful. And Nicholas, he didn't have the same chances of conception most men did. It was so unlikely.

Nicholas entered the room and smiled at her.

'Hey, you OK?' He put his arms around her.

'I'm fine. I just want to get out of here, Nick. Please take me home.' She buried her head in his chest inhaling the familiar fragrance of his body.

'I'll organise a car. The police want to speak to us, but I'll tell them to come to the house tomorrow. I think you've had enough excitement for one night.' He kissed the top of her head.

'I'm sorry I collapsed on you.' She wiped at her eyes and sat up to look at him.

'That's OK. It was a shock. I mean I am kind of used to you passing out if you've been on the tequila. But after a couple of beers, I knew something was wrong. You're made of sterner stuff than that.'

'D'you think it was my father? You know, who attacked Mike?' Freya asked him.

'Is that what *you* think?'

'I don't know.'

'Is that what made you have the anxiety attack? The thought of him being involved?'

'There's something I haven't told you.'

'Again? Is this about Jonny?'

'No. It isn't about Jonny.'

'Go on.'

'I got some hate mail in the post today. It was a letter, it just said the word "bitch", nothing else.'

'What?! Why didn't you tell me this morning?'

'I don't know. I should have, but we'd just made up and...'

'Freya, we need to talk to the police about this. Where is this note?'

'It was in my handbag. The one I left at the casino.'

'Right, well let's go home. I'm having Roger contact the security firm. Tomorrow morning I'm afraid we're having a new alarm system fitted, locks put on all the windows, a new front door, CCTV at the gate and...' he began.

'Oh no, Nick, no. I don't want our home turned into a fortress. Please.'

'I'm sorry, Freya. I'm not taking any chances anymore.'

Having somehow heard about the car attack on the journalists' grapevine, there were scores of photographers outside their home when they arrived back in Mayleaf.

'I'm going to get a bigger, higher gate put up and there will be no more making tea for the photographers either. You just don't know who you can trust.' He drove the car through the front gate and pulled up outside their door.

Freya didn't respond. She was still trying to take in the day's events. It was all too much to think about and she was tired. She just wanted to curl up in her own bed and go to sleep.

'So, did the doctor give you the all clear?' Nicholas asked.

'Yeah, I've had episodes like this before. I used to get them quite often when I lived with *him*.' She opened the car door.

'And you haven't told me that either. Why are you keeping this stuff to yourself? We're a team.' He followed her up the steps.

'I didn't tell you because it's embarrassing. You know the sort of person I am. I like to think I can take on the world and win. But the truth is, when the going really gets tough I freak out. Remember when Emma nearly lost the baby? I spent an hour at the hospital waiting for news about her, blowing into a paper bag, trying to keep a grip on things. That same night, when I told you who my father was, it was all I could do to get the story out without passing out.'

'Come on, let's get you inside and I'll make some tea.' He opened the front door.

Willis came bounding down the hallway to greet them both and started to weave himself in and out of Freya's legs as she tried to walk towards the kitchen.

'Hi, Willis,' she greeted.

Nicholas stopped in the doorway and turned around to face Freya. She knew just by looking at him something wasn't right.

'Hey, why don't you go and put on one of those trashy dramas you like watching and I'll make the tea.' He took her hand and started to lead her back up the hall.

'What's the matter? Why don't you want me going in the kitchen? I want to feed Willis.' She stood her ground.

'I'll feed him. You need to rest.'

'I need things to be normal again. That's what I need.' She brushed past Nicholas and entered the kitchen.

All around the room there were photographs. They covered all the worktops of the kitchen units. Some were stuck to the walls and the appliances and even the windows. They were photographs of her and Nicholas. Except they had been altered. Freya's face had been cut out of each and every picture.

'Oh my God, Nick!' Freya exclaimed. She put her hands to her face.

Nineteen

The bright light coming through the bedroom window woke Freya the following morning. Willis jumped up from his position at the bottom of the bed and walked all over her body to get to her face and lick it. Freya reached for her glasses and put them on. The bedside clock told her it was nine thirty.

Shocked by the time, she pulled back the duvet and leapt out of bed. She grabbed her robe and hurried out of the bedroom.

She ran down stairs and rushed into the kitchen, Willis struggling to keep up with her.

Nicholas was sat at the breakfast bar, reading through his script.

'Why didn't you wake me? I've got an appointment this morning.' She pulled open a cupboard and got out the cat food.

'I thought you could do with the sleep. It was gone two when the police left.'

'Well, that isn't going to change my appointment time is it? I'm never going to make it to the office in thirty minutes. I'm not even dressed.' She dropped the tin-opener on the floor.

'Hey, come on. I'll call Sasha. I'll tell her you're not coming in today. She can see to the appointments.' He stood up and picked up the tin-opener.

'I *want* to go in today. I want to go in and pretend none of this is happening.' She started to open the can.

'Come on, Freya. Sit down, have some tea. Willis is playing you by the way, I've already fed him this morning. Come, sit down.' He took her arm and guided her towards the breakfast bar.

'I just feel like I want to press rewind on the last couple of days and re-record.' She put her elbows on the table, resting her head in her hands.

'It hasn't been the best, but we have the police involved now. Then Roger's coming over later to see to the new security arrangements.'

'Nick, I don't want to be locked in this house with infrared beams and cameras and a portcullis coming down at the front door. That isn't living.'

'Someone's been in this house, Freya and I think they've been in this house before. I don't think that crow hit the glass in the door. I think someone broke in. You saw the pictures, whoever it was destroyed every photo we ever had taken. What if defacing things isn't enough for them? I'm not putting you at risk.'

'Well you may as well shoot me now, because I'm not living like that.'

'I know you're mad at me because I told the police about your father, but it had to be done. If you really think this is down to him then they have to investigate it.'

'Then things are going to get much worse. There's one thing my father hates more than me and that's the cops. Once they start sniffing around his offices, asking questions there will be hell to pay.'

'Hey, come on, have some tea. There's still left over Chinese from yesterday's left over Chinese in the fridge. Do you want me to microwave it for you?'

'Have we got any honey?'

'I don't think so. Although I think there's some peanut butter if you're thinking of a spread.'

'Do we have Jell-O? Can I have toast with Jell-O?'

'If I can find Jell-O it's yours.'

'If I don't go into the office will you stay at home with me?'

'Of course I will. Maybe, to take our mind off things, we can start making the wedding arrangements,' he suggested.

'Yeah, maybe.' She smiled but her heart wasn't in it.

'Right, well, why don't you go and get showered and I'll make this Jell-O on toast thing you want.'

'OK, I won't be long.' She left the kitchen and headed up the hallway. She stopped in her tracks when she heard Nicholas pick up the phone.

'Hey, Sandra it's Nick. Listen, I want you to make an appointment for me. Yeah, I want you to telephone Lawson-Peck Industries and get me a meeting with Eric Lawson-Peck. Don't take no for an answer. I want it as soon as possible.'

What the hell was he doing?

Roger and the security company arrived a little after ten thirty. They had four trucks and a team of fifteen people. When they'd unloaded the vehicles and started to get out all manner of locks, bolts and alarms it began to look like a locksmiths' convention. It was too much for Freya. She kept herself busy making cups of tea.

'This is the plan I've come up with. If you want to have a look and see what you think. Then the guys can get started installing everything,' Roger said. He passed the plans over to Nicholas.

'And this will definitely keep anyone out? It's guaranteed? I mean, Freya does have a habit of forgetting to set the alarm and...' he started.

'This equipment is state of the art. You can't leave the house without knowing you haven't activated it. It warns you with a noise and a verbal command and it won't let you leave until you've done what it says.'

'It won't let you leave until you've done what it says?! What is this machine based on? *Terminator*?' Freya exclaimed. She put a pot of tea on the table.

'It sounds complicated but it's really simple to use. I'll go through it all with you when it's up and running,' Roger assured.

'I have a better idea. Why don't we *not* install it and move to a desert island where the only things to bother us would be sun, sea and fish?'

'Excuse Freya, Roger. She's not had a lot of sleep and what with what happened to Mike. She's understandably edgy.'

'Don't make excuses for me. I'm just bordering on being admitted as a psych patient that's all.' She slammed a plate of biscuits down.

She was actually bordering on fury. Nicholas hadn't mentioned anything about arranging to meet her father. So much for there being no more secrets! He knew how scared she was of her father. He ought to believe her when she said he was dangerous. Meeting him, having a head on confrontation was madness.

The phone rang and Nicholas jumped up to answer it.

'He won't even let me answer the phone now. God knows what he thinks is going to happen if I *do* answer it.'

Of course, it could also be because he was waiting for a call back from Sandra arranging the meeting with her father.

'He's worried for you, Freya. *I'm* worried for you too. Having someone get into your house like that and do a crazy thing…it's unsettling,' Roger told her.

'It's Sasha for you.' Nicholas held the phone out to her.

'Shit, I forgot to ring her. Hello, Sasha. Did Mrs Garcia turn up? I'm so sorry, I meant to ring you to cancel her and…'

'It's fine, she came and I saw her. She's booked a session with you next week,' Sasha spoke.

Freya moved out into the hall.

'Oh thanks, Sasha. That was great of you.'

'So are you coming in to the office today?'

'Er no, not today. We had a bit of a time of it last night. Nick's driver got attacked by this gang and the car was smashed up. Then when we got home last night someone had been in our house.'

Saying it out loud made her realise how bad this situation had become.

'No! How awful! Was it a robbery?' Sasha exclaimed.

'We don't exactly know yet. Anyway, the police are investigating and we have a security team here this morning making sure no one will be getting in here again. You should see them, they're so hi-tech they could probably build the Starship Enterprise.'

'Well, that must have been awful, having someone in your house like that. Did they take anything?"

'We haven't had a chance to go through everything yet, but it doesn't look like it.'

'Well, that's something. So, I expect you're both feeling a bit shaken up.'

'A bit, but we can't let it take over our lives. After all, we have a wedding to organise.'

'Of course! Are you still planning to go ahead with it on December twenty second? Have you thought more about venues?'

'We can't make up our minds at the moment, but when we do you'll be one of the first to know.'

'OK, well don't worry about anything here. I'll get Avril in if I need her and field anything I can't deal with personally.'

'Thanks, Sasha, I'll see you tomorrow. Oh one thing you should know. I lost my handbag last night, so if you need to call you'll have to phone this number. My mobile was in there.'

'Oh, OK. I will.'

'See you.'

She went back into the kitchen where Roger and Nicholas were discussing where to put the motion sensors.

'Could I make a suggestion?' Freya asked.

'Sure,' Roger replied.

'I don't think having motion sensors in the bedroom would be a good idea. I don't want half of Mayleaf woken up every night thinking there's an air strike about to happen if the alarm goes off.'

'Roger will tell you all about motion sensors later. They have an on and off button. That means every room in the house is open for experimentation.' He winked at Freya.

'Ah, jeez! Guys! Trying to think security here and anyway, you aren't even married yet,' Roger reminded them.

'But we will be soon.' Nicholas put his arms around Freya and kissed her on the mouth.

'Nick, can we go out for lunch today? Maybe get a takeout from Casey's and go and see one of the bridges?' Freya asked, turning to face him.

'Sure, is that OK, Roger? You don't need me here for anything do you?'

'No, if you're happy with the plan, the team can get on with it. It'll take them most of the day to install everything. As long as you're back this evening for me to explain everything to you then that's fine. I have your cell, I can call.'

'By the way, Roger, what are all these alarms and beams and motion sensors going to mean for Willis?' Freya wanted to know.

'Yeah I've thought of that. Willis might be a problem. We might have to train him to limbo.'

Nicholas laughed out loud.

'I was being serious!'

'Yeah I know you were, babe. Don't worry, we're going to take care of it.'

Twenty

Freya was glad to get out of the house. The security team seemed to be in every corner of her home and it was unnerving the amount of measuring, pointing and drilling they were doing. She didn't really relax until they were at County Bridge.

They'd bought bagels, sodas and a mud pie from Casey's and they took the food down to the bridge. They sat together, their feet hanging over the side, watching the water flow up stream.

'God, it's been a mad few days,' Nicholas remarked, taking a sip of his drink.

'Completely mad.'

'Look, Freya I know we agreed we'd try and live like two normal people, with no ostentatious behaviour or unnecessary, showy outings. We also said we'd involve ourselves in the community and try and become a part of that…' he started.

'I'm waiting for the "but". Did I interrupt it? Was the "but" coming just then?'

'I just want you to know I don't want the security either. I love living in Mayleaf. We have a real home there with friends who care about us. I don't think I've ever felt as at home anywhere as I do there. Perhaps it's a sign of getting old, but when I have to leave to film or something, I really don't want to go.'

'No, I feel the same. That's why I hate that this is happening. It's spoiling everything.'

'We'll try not to let it ruin things but we have to take precautions. We would be crazy not to.'

'I know, Nick, I'm not stupid. I know we have to be careful and that, like it or not, we're on the top of the celebrity tree. I just never asked for it that's all. The attention, the spotlight, that's *your* thing not mine,' Freya reminded him.

'I would never do anything to put you in any danger and if my chosen career is putting you in danger, putting *us* in danger then…'

'It isn't *you* putting us in danger, it's my father. And don't you dare say you would give it up because I will *not* let you do that. You love what you do and you're fantastic at it. And look at everything we've achieved in the last six months or so. We've donated more money to worthy causes than anyone else on the planet.'

'But at what price? If this isn't your father's work then it's the work of someone who obviously doesn't care for us much.' He took a sip of his drink.

'Doesn't care for *me* much you mean. You weren't headless in any of the pictures.'

'I was just going to say maybe we should step out of the limelight for a while. I don't know, maybe your desert island idea wasn't such a joke after all.'

'I have so much going on right now, with the Every Day project, not to mention my photography exhibition coming up. I couldn't hide away even if I wanted to. I can't start something and then abandon it. Anyway, stepping away from things would be like giving in to my father wouldn't it? You know he scares the shit out of me, but you also know I hate giving in to anyone.' She bit into her bagel.

'I just want to protect you, Freya. As alpha male as that sounds. I don't want to have brought you over here and made your life a misery.'

And now would be an excellent time to mention meeting with her father. Was he going to tell her? Or was he going to keep it from her? She paused long, met his eyes with hers. Nothing was forthcoming.

'Nick, you've made me so happy, so unbelievably happy. Every morning I wake up lying next to this Adonis and I can't believe my luck. I keep thinking someone's going to produce some ruby slippers from somewhere, click the heels together three times and have me whirlwinding back to Clapham. I love you, Nick, so much.' She took hold of his hand.

'I love you too.' He reached out and gently touched her face, drawing her towards him to kiss her.

'Listen, if you want to hold off on the wedding I would understand,' he said.

'Is that what you want?' Freya asked him.

'Hell no! I want to marry you now more than ever.'

'Then let's do it.' She nodded with determination.

'Where?'

'Anywhere, I don't care. Casey's? Statue of Liberty? Bungee jumping over the Grand Canyon? You choose.' She laughed.

Breaking the moment, Nicholas' phone began to ring.

'Argh! You said you'd turned it off. I can't be marrying someone who can't be separated from their mobile phone.' She jumped up.

'I can't be married to someone who can't be separated from their cameras. I see Claude under your t-shirt and I also saw you sneak Max into the car,' Nicholas called to her.

'Pervert! You're nothing but a dirty voyeur, watching my every move.' She set off across the bridge.

'It's Sandra, I'll catch you up.'

She waved her hand at him and Nicholas put the phone to his ear.

'Hello, Sandra…you did? Good. Yes, tonight's fine. What time and where? Eight at the President's Lounge? Yeah, I know where it is. OK, thanks. I'll see you.'

She wasn't stupid. She knew this was the call he'd been waiting all morning for. She just wished he wasn't hiding it from her. There was no way she was going to let him go anywhere near her father.

'Smile!' she called, focusing her camera on him.

'Freya, that was Sandra. I've got to do an interview tonight at eight on some chat show on the Film Factor Network. It was supposed to be next week but they want to tape it tonight so…'

Freya let out a heavy sigh and shook her head at him.

'What's wrong? Why are you looking at me like that?'

"I know you're planning to meet my father. I heard you this morning. And now you're lying to me about it. We said no more secrets and you're making up some bullshit about going to do a show when you're planning on putting yourself in a room with that madman.'

Nicholas held up his hands in defeat.

'You can phone Sandra back right now and tell her to cancel. I won't let you go and see him.' She sniffed, tried to stop the tears from being created.

'Freya, I'm sorry I lied but I'm not sorry I made the appointment. I have to sort this out.'

'No.'

'It's not your decision to make. He's hurting both of us now. I'm in this, just as much of you and I want it to stop. He's not going to control our lives. He's not going to hurt the people we care about. And he's not going to drive a wedge between us.' He slammed his hand down on the bridge.

'Nick, you don't understand…'

'No. I've heard enough about it. I'm going to see him, Freya. I'm going to see him and I'm going to end this.'

'But…'

'No. No buts. End of conversation.'

Twenty One

'Freya, where the hell have you been all day? Why haven't you been answering your mobile?!'

She tried to swallow the hunk of cheese she had in her mouth so she could speak.

'Freya! Are you there?' Emma questioned.

'Mmm…hang on. Sorry about that. What did you say?' She swiped at her mouth with her hands.

'I've been trying to get hold of you all day. It's all over the news about your car being attacked and Mike being hurt and something happening at your house. What's going on?'

'Sorry it's all been a bit crazy here. I lost my bag with my phone in at the casino and it hasn't been turned in, so don't be surprised if you end up getting a phone call from some drifter.'

'Are you OK?'

'Not really. We had an intruder in the house. We got home after the car incident last night to find the kitchen covered in photographs of me and Nick. Well, I say me and Nick, they were of Nick really because someone had done some sloppy editing of me with a pair of scissors.'

'What?! Oh my God!'

'I have to say it wasn't the best welcome home I've had. But Roger and an army of security experts have made my lovely little Waltonesque house into something that now resembles Alcatraz.'

'Oh, Freya. Do you think it has something to do with the article about your father?'

'Do I think it has something to do with my rich, lowlife, daughter-hating father? Can I ask the audience?' She sucked in a breath and thought about Nicholas. He'd left an hour ago. They were hardly talking to each other. He'd never been so bloody minded like he had today at the bridge. She was worried about him. She'd seen people after an audience with her father. She didn't know if she could tell Emma about it.

'And Mike's attack? God, do you think he did that too?'

'I'd say it was an incident right out of the psychotic father book of "Ways to Bring People to their Knees".'

'Did you tell the police you think it's him?'

'No I didn't, but Nick did.' She swallowed a lump in her throat. She couldn't say the words. She couldn't tell Emma she'd let her fiancé go to face her father.

'Nick's worried about me, he's gone all Neanderthal actually. I've got Jolie coming round to keep me company because Nick's...had to go out and he doesn't want to leave me alone.' She took the slab of cheese out of the fridge and sunk her teeth into it.

She moved into the hallway and headed for the living room.

'I think he's right to be protective. You've had someone in your house, that's terrible and freaky and I can't imagine how jumpy I would be in that situation.'

'Thanks, Em, that's made me feel a whole lot better about the whole thing. I was so trying not to feel like the babysitter in a horror movie but now...'

'Sorry, but I'm worried about you too. When are you coming over here? Perhaps the sooner the better would be best. Have you made any wedding arrangements yet?'

'Er, no, not really. There hasn't been time, what with police and psychos and motion sensors. Say, what's been happening in Kassiopi? Tell me about stuff there to take my mind off it.' She sat down on the sofa and took another bite of cheese.

'Oh there's nothing happening here this time of year. The holiday season doesn't kick in until May, so everything is quiet...and not so warm.'

'Don't talk to me about warm. I moved to America to catch some rays and they're talking about snow here next week! Snow! I know it's November but snow?!'

'I'd love to see snow.'

'The wind here would kill you. Anyway, how's everyone? How are Mr and Mrs P?'

Mr and Mrs Petroholis were Emma's parents in law. They were good, honest people who thought the world of Freya.

'Everyone's fine. Why do I get the impression you're hiding something from me?'

'What? No, I'm not. I just want to try and focus on something else other than what's going on here. Tell me about the building work with your house. Are those Greek builders still on schedule?'

Emma wouldn't give up until she'd confessed everything. She couldn't tell her about Nicholas meeting her father. The less people knew about that the better.

'Freya.'

'Alright, alright, I've been in hospital. I passed out at the casino when I found out about Mike.'

She took another bite of cheese.

'I knew it. It's those dizzy spells you used to get because of your father wasn't it?'

'I guess. I think it freaked Nick out a bit. Apparently I did the whole rolling eyes, white sweaty face, collapsing on the floor thing.'

'What did the doctor say?'

'He said I'm pregnant.' She laughed.

'What?!'

'Oh apparently they did some obviously flawed blood test and it showed up something or other. I told him, there is no way I can be pregnant.'

'Freya, what are you saying? The doctor told you you're pregnant and you don't believe him?'

'Of course I don't believe him. What I think happened is that they mixed up my results with some other poor woman. She could be going out and getting drunk right now with no knowledge of her unborn child.'

'Well, what did the doctor say when you told him you didn't think you were pregnant?'

'Oh he said something about a scan to check, but I wasn't having that. I mean, I'd just woken up from some horrible debilitating sedative they'd given me and I just wanted to get out of there.'

'Freya, I think you have to go back to the hospital and have a scan. Doctors don't tell you you're pregnant for no reason and hospitals mixing up results doesn't happen very often. You're pregnant.'

'I'm *not* pregnant! Me! Pregnant! Don't be stupid! The whole idea of it is just completely mad! Nick and I are careful you know. And although the hospital says he can have children, he hasn't got the full kit has he? The chances have to be slimmer.'

'What's so mad about the idea of you being pregnant?'

'Em, the first couple of weeks we had Willis I forgot to feed him three times. When Nick wasn't here he had to leave Post-Its on the fridge to remind me,' Freya told her.

'And you think you'd do the same with a baby? Well, let me tell you, the noise they make you wouldn't be able to forget it's there,' Emma assured her.

'Well, that's another thing. I mean, I like my sleep and I don't function very well without it. From what I know about babies that isn't a good combination.'

'Have you done a test yourself?'

'No!'

'Well, why not? If you're so sure you aren't pregnant, do a test.'

'It would be a waste of money. I mean I could probably buy about five or six large bars of chocolate for the price of a test.'

'It sounds to me like you're in denial. Buy a test, pee on the stick and then you'll know. But if you don't want to waste chocolate money go and see the doctor again, get a scan.'

'You know me and hospitals.'

'You can't just do nothing. What does Nick say about it?'

'Got to go, Em, that's the intercom buzzing. It'll be Jolie.' She stood up and marched up and down to replicate movement.

'Freya! Don't you dare go! You haven't spoken to Nick about it, have you?! Freya! Don't you hang up on me!'

'Sorry, Em, Jolie's here. I'll call you tomorrow.'

Freya looked at the lump of cheese in her hand and saw she had consumed half of it. She couldn't be pregnant, not now, possibly not ever. She hadn't ever thought about it properly. It had never been high on her priority list. She suspected it had something to do with her childhood. She had nothing good to take from her life as a child to pass on to anyone else.

Suddenly there was a loud bang from the kitchen and the alarm system began going off. The deafening wail had Freya leaping up and covering her ears, not knowing what to do.

Her heart was racing and she just stood still frozen to the spot.

The phone began to ring and she just looked at it, not knowing whether to pick up. With the alarm blaring, she took a deep breath and answered the call.

'Hello.'

'Please identify yourself. This is the police. We've been alerted to the alarm activation.' The voice barked at her, sharp and commanding.

'Um, I'm Freya Johnson. There was a noise from the kitchen and then the alarm went off and...'

The lightheadedness was there again. Her eyes couldn't focus.

'Password!' the voice barked again.

'Um, I, er, just give me a minute...'

She felt like she was going to vomit. She couldn't remember what her password was.

'You have twenty seconds then I'll radio for an immediate armed response.'

'Um, er, it's "John McClane". Did you hear that? John McClane!'

As soon as the words were out of her mouth, the noise of the alarm ceased.

'Hello, Miss Johnson, my name is Vanessa. I've deactivated the alarm here, but you will need to reset the control panel. Now, are you sure everything's OK?' the woman's voice spoke.

'I think so. I don't know, I think I'm deaf. Let me go and check the kitchen.'

Gingerly she left the lounge and made her way up the hallway towards the kitchen.

She flipped on the light and saw Willis in the middle of the kitchen, stood next to a black crow, feathers around his lips. Freya looked up from the floor and saw the kitchen window was broken and glass was all over the work top.

'I think you'd better get the police to come.' She called Willis to her and picked him up.

'OK, Miss Johnson, I'll have a unit come straight over. Do you want to keep talking to me until they arrive?'

The intercom buzzed loudly and it startled her. Her breath caught in her throat and she almost let go of Willis and the phone. Willis jumped from her arms.

'Miss Johnson, is everything OK?'

'Yes, yes it's fine. Hang on, just one second. Hello?' she said into the intercom system.

'Hi, Freya, it's Jolie,' her neighbour's voice called through the speaker.

'Hi, Jolie. Come on up to the house. Er, hello? Vanessa? It's fine, it's my neighbour. She'll be here until the police arrive. Thank you for your help.'

She ended the call and rushed through the hallway to the front door to meet Jolie. She could see her friend marching up the driveway laden down with grocery bags.

'Sorry I'm late, Freya. Adrian decided to paint the kitchen with ketchup and...well look at your hair!' Jolie said.

'I...well...I've got the police coming in a second and...'

'You haven't had another break in! Oh my God, when?! With you here in the house?' She went up the steps to the house.

'Well, it wasn't really a break in, it was…look come in and make yourself at home. I've got some wine open and there's beer in the fridge or there's soda or…I've just got to call someone about the broken window.'

'I'll do that.' Jolie put her arm around Freya. 'I'll also make some tea.'

Twenty Two

The President's Lounge was a well-known members only club in California. It was frequented by the rich and famous and was very exclusive. Nicholas had been a member for some years, but he'd only been in the establishment once when he'd met with a director. It wasn't his scene.

He nodded to a few people he recognised and made his way to the bar at the far end of the room. He didn't like the place. It was all bright lights and wall-to-wall names from the American edition of *Who's Who*. It wasn't somewhere he felt comfortable.

He ordered a beer from the bartender and sat down.

'Hello, Mr Kaden. How are you? We haven't seen you here for some time,' the barman greeted with a smile.

'Try about five years.'

'How's everything with you?'

'Good thanks. Listen, I'm meant to be meeting with Eric Lawson-Peck tonight. Has he arrived yet?'

'Sure. He's in his office. It's on the fourth floor.'

'His office?'

'Yes.' The barman put a bottle of beer on the bar.

'His office?' Nicholas repeated.

'Yes. Mr Lawson-Peck owns the President's Lounge. Take the door at the end of this room and take the lift to the fourth floor.'

Nicholas took a swig of his beer then crossed the room.

He caught the lift and when the doors opened there were two large black men, dressed in tuxedos, stood outside waiting for him.

'Mr Kaden,' the larger of the two men greeted.

'Hey.'

'If you wouldn't mind removing all the metal you're carrying and holding your arms out. Just for a weapons check.'

'A weapons check?'

'Yes, sir, it's just routine. If you wouldn't mind.' The smaller man produced a scanning machine.

Nicholas took off his watch and removed his car keys from his pocket. He handed them to the large man then held his arms out for the smaller man to run the machine up, down and around him like a wand.

The machine let out a loud beep.

'A belt buckle. Sorry, forgot.'

The smaller man parted the jacket of Nicholas' suit and revealed the offending item. He then patted Nicholas down from shoulders to toe and even looked inside his socks.

'Thank you, Mr Kaden. It's this way.' The larger man gave Nicholas his valuables back.

The two men led him down the corridor and they stopped at a thick set of double doors. The larger man pressed a button and spoke into an intercom.

'Mr Lawson-Peck, I have Mr Kaden. Are you ready for him?'

There was silence for a time and then the reply came.

'Show him in, Fraser.'

There was a buzz. Fraser, pushed open the door and the smaller man indicated for Nicholas to follow, while he brought up the rear.

He stepped into the room. There were glass windows at the far end, with a fantastic view of the city below. A big desk sat just in front of that, with a chair either side and a bookcase full of leather-bound books on one wall. There was no one else there.

'Wait here,' Fraser ordered, pulling out the chair from the desk.

Nicholas did as he was told and sat down while the two men went back through the room and left.

He was just contemplating standing back up again when a sudden movement to his right made him turn. The bookcase rotated and Eric Lawson-Peck appeared in the room.

Nicholas had only ever seen the man in photographs and there was nothing striking about his appearance. He was of average height, approximately five foot ten. He had receding, fair hair that was greying at the temples and he was slimly built. He was wearing a dark blue designer suit, his shirt open at the neck and no tie.

Eric paused momentarily and then walked swiftly towards his desk and sat down opposite Nicholas.

Eric placed his hands on the desk and then suddenly stood up again and outstretched his hand in Nicholas' direction.

'I don't believe we've ever met.'

'No, I don't believe we have. I would've remembered,' Nicholas responded, unmoving.

Eric smiled and sat back down in his chair.

'So, to what do I owe the pleasure?' Eric opened a drawer of his desk and took out a box of cigars.

'I would have thought that was obvious.'

'Not to me. Would you like one?' He offered the cigars across the table.

'No thank you. I don't.'

'Oh, that's right. You had cancer didn't you? How stupid of me! Someone who's had cancer wouldn't want to be taking any unnecessary risks would they?' Eric lit his cigar and drew on it, producing a fog of smoke.

'Look, Eric, we both know why I'm here...' Nicholas started.

'Thank you. I'd be delighted,' the older man interrupted.

'What?'

'Your marriage to my daughter. I would be delighted to come. I take it you *have* brought an invitation.'

Nicholas let out a sigh.

'That isn't why you're here? Well then, I'm at a loss as to why you *are* here.'

'You know why. Ever since the paper printed that article about Freya telling someone you were dead, everything's started to go to shit for her again. Just like it did the last time you involved yourself in her life,' Nicholas snapped.

'I have absolutely no idea what you're talking about.'

'Come on. Don't play the innocent with me. I'm an actor, remember? I can smell an act and you don't fool me. You can't bear it that everyone's questioning you again. Snooping into your world, wanting to know why Freya doesn't want to have you anywhere near her. Wondering again if the other article you bullied her into changing was actually true.'

'I'll tell you something shall I? I don't much care for people getting the police around my property in the early hours of the morning, waking me up and asking pointless questions. I don't much care for people who bandy my name around all over the place and spout malicious lies about me. I do not care for people who show me no respect.' Eric leaned forward in his chair, his arms on the desk.

'And I don't much care for people who beat up my driver, break into my home and send my fiancée obscene letters.'

Eric smiled and sat back in his chair.

'Do you know, Nick? May I call you Nick? Perhaps I should, seeing as how we're almost family. Do you know I was actually surprised Jane managed to keep her anonymity for so long. At the end of the day though, it's always the same old story with her. She just can't keep her mouth shut.'

'Her name isn't Jane anymore. She hasn't been Jane for a long time. Her name is *Freya* and the reason *Freya* can't keep her mouth shut, as you so eloquently put it, is because she can't forget what you put her through.'

'Have you ever considered, Nick, that maybe Jane's been embellishing things? I mean she does have a habit of doing that, doesn't she? Perhaps she's still feeling a little aggrieved I sent her to prison. I mean that might just give someone an axe to grind, don't you think?'

'What are you trying to say? That you didn't beat Freya quite as hard as she tells people you did? That she hid in her wardrobe *less* times than she claims? There has to be truth at the beginning for it to be embellished.'

'Your fiancée needs to learn some self restraint, particularly when the press is around. I was sure that'd be something you'd have taught her by now. I've seen you work the journalists, avoid the tricky questions, change the direction of conversation. I have no doubt you know when to make no comment.'

'If you knew Freya at all then you'd know she's her own person and no one tells her what to do, least of all me.'

'Well, well, what is this? You're admitting you're not the master of your own household? I'm surprised at you, Nick.' He took a long, slow drag of his cigar.

'We share things, Eric. That's how a relationship should work. There shouldn't be a tyrant handing out orders with a firm hand and a sharp tongue. That behaviour doesn't make you a man, it makes you a bully.'

Eric smiled and nodded, resting his cigar in the ashtray on the desk. Nicholas swallowed. Eric thumped his hands down on the desk and leaned towards Nicholas, his lips curled into a snarl.

'How dare you come into my office, sit there and insult me! I thought better of you. I thought you might have a little respect for me. I didn't think you were foolish enough to try and pick an argument with me,' Eric hissed.

'You don't frighten me. Look at yourself! A small man in a flash suit, hiding behind a big desk and two, even bigger, security guards. Appearing from behind a false bookcase! What was that all about? Who do you see yourself as, Eric? Some kind of Bond villain?' He held firm in his seat.

'If I were you I'd keep that smart mouth of yours in check. I have a feeling you've been with Jane for too long. Some of her acridness has rubbed off on you.'

'The only people you attack are those you think are smaller and weaker than you. I am *not* one of them.'

'What makes you think I won't finish you right here and now?' Eric wanted to know.

'You don't have it in you. You don't sully your own hands. You pay people to do it for you.'

'Not when it's personal.'

'Listen, you can do whatever you like to me. You can have me assaulted, have me killed if you must, but leave Freya alone. She's suffered enough.'

'You'd put yourself in the firing line for her. How touching.'

'I love her. I would do absolutely anything in my power to protect her. That's why I'm here now. Don't think for a moment I really want to be anywhere near you, let alone in the same room as you. You disgust me.'

'It's a funny thing isn't it? What disgusts people. I mean, what's your definition of disgusting, Nick?' Eric queried. He sat back in his seat and picked up the cigar again.

'What are you talking about? I don't have time for this. I've said what I came to say.' He stood up, turned away.

'Sit down!' Eric ordered.

'Go to hell! I'm not answerable to you.' He headed towards the door.

'Oh, trust me, Nick. You'll want to hear this.'

Nicholas turned back round to face him.

'Please, sit back down. I think you'll need to.'

'I'm not in to playing games.' He walked back to the desk and Eric.

'I understand you've met my son.' He relit his cigar and raised his eyes to meet Nicholas'.

'I'm sorry, you've lost me.'

'You met my son, the other day. Now, he's a fine boy, almost a chip off the old block. I mean he has definitely inherited my business brain. He's rich and successful and he's going places. In fact the only defect he has is a rather pathetic weakness in the emotional department,' Eric told him.

'I'm still not with you. I didn't know you had a son.'

'No, well, it isn't something I've broadcast. In this case, all parties concerned have kept their mouths shut. But despite his rather unsavoury conception, he's turned out rather well. His name's Jonathan by the way. I believe Jane still calls him Jonny.'

'Oh my God.' He took a breath and moistened his lips.

'I did say you'd want to stay and hear it, didn't I? So, now who's disgusting, Nick? Jane for sleeping with her half-brother? Or me for parting them when I could?'

'My God. This is sick. *You* are sick. I don't believe a word of it.' Nicholas rose from his seat.

'You'd better believe it, because he's the only reason I'm not having you and Jane wiped off the face of the planet. He came to me. He heard about your driver's little incident and he begged me, he pleaded with me to leave his sister alone. It was pathetic. It was utter weakness. He was sniveling and groveling and it made me feel nauseous. And do you know? Despite everything, I think he still loves her. It's a little frightening considering their genealogy, but I suppose deep feelings never leave you do they?' Eric continued.

'If you are lying about this, I swear to God I'll kill you.'

'Empty threats bore me, Nick. No, it's the truth. Jane has a half-brother. Her ex-fiancé.'

'Is he planning on telling her? Because he's just pledged a whole stack of money to her charity.'

'Is he planning on telling her? Well, he was sworn to silence by me until I lifted that bar about…ooo, it must be an hour ago now. His begging and pleading hit a nerve with me. Perhaps I'm getting sentimental in my old age. I told him I'd leave you and Jane alone…on the condition he told her the truth about his parentage. I thought that news should be just enough to ruin her wedding day and more importantly your wedding *night*. I mean, how is she going to feel knowing she's slept with her brother?' Eric smiled a smug, self-satisfied grin.

'You are one sick fuck, do you know that?'

'You can leave now. You know where the door is.' He dropped his gaze and picked up some paperwork from the desk.

'Stay away from me and stay away from Freya, or I promise you, I will make you pay,' Nicholas warned. He stood up, fixed his eyes on Eric.

'Goodbye, Nick. I would say it's been a treat. But, well…it hasn't.'

'The feeling's mutual.' Nicholas headed for the door.

'Oh, and by the way, just so we're clear about things. I don't waste my time sending threatening notes. I find actions usually work best. So, whoever has it in for Jane on that score, it isn't me. Letters, they're so amateur.'

Nicholas didn't reply. He pulled open the door and left the office.

Twenty Three

'Thanks for coming, Roger and for organising the glazier. I do appreciate it,' Freya spoke.

The police had been and gone, the glazier had fixed the broken window and Freya and Roger were rejoining Jolie in the living room with fresh drinks and nibbles.

'It isn't a problem. Stop thanking me. I'm just surprised someone got over that fence that's all,' Roger said. He sat down in an armchair.

'Oh don't! I know exactly what Nick is going to say when he gets home. He's going to say *that's it, we have to have the electric fence back*. Jolie, we had this twenty foot high electric fence at our old house and it was so ugly. The birds kept getting electrocuted when they landed on it and...' Freya began.

'She's exaggerating. They got slightly singed.' Roger laughed.

'It was cruel and it was like living in a compound. Like Guantanamo Bay or something.'

'I'm not sure I'd like one around my home,' Jolie admitted as she helped herself to some potato chips.

'I know you have reservations about them, but it's one sure way of almost guaranteeing no one can get in here again,' Roger stated.

'Notice he said "almost" guaranteeing,' Freya said to Jolie.

'Well, the only way someone could get in would be if there was a major power out, or if it was turned off from the inside.'

'Oh, enough! I don't want to talk about security anymore tonight. We have *Moonlighting* to get through yet.' Freya got up and headed towards the DVD player.

The intercom buzzed.

'Do you want me to get that?' Roger asked, standing up.

'No, don't be silly. I'll go. Start the DVD without me. I've seen them all before, I'll catch up.' Freya left the room.

She went into the kitchen and pressed the connection button.

'Hello.'

'Hi, Freya. It's Jonathan.'

'Oh, Jonny. What are you doing here? It's late and…'

'Can I come in? I really need to speak with you. It's important,' he interrupted.

'Well, I have friends here. It's not really a good time. Can't we do this tomorrow?' She looked at her watch. She had hoped Nicholas would be back by now. She should have stopped him. What if Eric had done something?

'No, it can't wait. I need to talk to you tonight. I wouldn't be here right now if it wasn't absolutely necessary.'

'Oh, OK. I'm opening the gate. Come on up to the house.'

She hurried back into the living room, told Roger and Jolie she had someone coming about a business matter and went to the door.

He was just getting out of his car when Freya opened it. He looked awful. He was wearing a suit but it was crumpled. His shirt was hanging out and he wasn't wearing a tie. His hair was ruffled and his beard was untrimmed.

'Hi.' His greeting was lacklustre.

'Hi. Are you OK? You look terrible.'

'I've just had a difficult meeting that's all. I could do with a drink though. Is that OK?' He looked uncomfortable and started to tuck his shirt into his trousers.

'Sure. Come on in.' Freya stepped aside to let him pass by into her home.

'I'm sorry to barge in on your evening like this, but I didn't think this could wait until morning,' he said as they made their way into the kitchen.

'That's OK. Jolie and Roger are amusing themselves with Bruce Willis. We're good for half an hour or so.' She smiled. 'Wine? Beer? Or tea?'

'Beer would be good. So, is Nick not here?'

'No. Not at the moment. I'm expecting him back soon though.'

If her father hadn't hurt him. No, she shouldn't think like that. There was CCTV everywhere these days and Nicholas wasn't stupid.

'He missed all the drama again. I had another broken window,' Freya told him. She pointed at it.

'What happened? Are you OK?'

'Someone broke the window and dumped another dead bird on the floor. If it wasn't so freaky I'd thank them. Willis is lapping it up…literally.' She passed him a bottle of beer.

'Willis?'

'Our mad cat.'

'Oh.'

He seemed disinterested and distracted.

'Are you sure you're OK? Sit down.' She pulled out a stool from under the breakfast bar.

'God, Freya. I just don't know how to do this.' He let out a weighted sigh.

'Oh no! You're going to pull your support from the Every Day project, aren't you?' She put her hands to her mouth, anticipating bad news.

'What? No. No, not at all. It's nothing to do with the project.'

The phone rang.

'Do you mind if I get that? It might be Nick.'

Jonathan shrugged. He took a swig of his beer and wiped his mouth with his hand.

'Hello.'

'Freya, it's Nick. Are you OK?'

'Are *you* OK?'

It was so good to hear his voice.

'I'm fine.'

'Did Roger call you? I told him not to.'

'Roger? No. Why? Has something happened?'

'Oh, someone broke a window and flung in a dead crow again.'

'What?! Again! Is Roger there now? Have you called the police?'

'Nick, calm down. I can hear you're driving. I called the police. They've been. The window's fixed and Roger said he'd stay until you got home. He's getting to know Jolie in the company of Bruce and Cybill while I talk to Jonny.' She looked to her companion. 'He's just turned up, looking like shit I might add, and he's acting a bit weird. I think it's woman trouble.' She smiled and winked at Jonathan.

'Jonny's there?'

'Yeah, he just turned up.' She moved with the phone, out of the kitchen and into the hallway.

'I want to speak with him.'

'Nick, is something wrong? Haven't we been through the jealousy thing already? He isn't undressing me with his eyes or any other part of his anatomy. He isn't even flirting with me yet.'

'Freya, please. Let me speak with him. Put Jonny on, Freya. Now. It's important.'

She walked back into the kitchen and held out the phone to Jonathan.

'Nick wants to speak to you.'

Jonathan took the phone and put it to his ear.

'Hello.'

'Listen, I know why you're there and you are *not* going to tell her anything. Do you hear me?'

'I don't know what you mean.' He forced a smile at Freya.

'You know exactly what I mean. Don't piss me off, Jonny! I know all about it. I've just been to see your father.'

'Uh huh. Is that so?'

'I do not want you to tell her. I mean it. If anyone's telling her this, it's me. Have you got that?'

'I don't think I can let you do that. I think I need to explain things for myself.'

'If you tell her she might never be the same again. How the hell d'you think she's going to feel about this?'

'How do you think *I* feel? How do you think *I've* been feeling?'

'I am begging you, Jonny. If you feel anything for her, you'll leave this to me.'

'I'm sorry. I can't.'

Twenty Four

'What's going on, Jonny? Why did Nick want to speak to you?'

'Freya, there's something I have to tell you. I should have told you from the start, back when I first found out. But I was scared and my mother was scared, so I blocked it out and tried to put it out of my mind... ignore it if you like.'

'I have no idea what you're talking about but you're starting to worry me.'

'God, this is hard. I don't know where to start.' He let out a sigh and put his hands into the pockets of his trousers.

'The beginning is usually a good place.'

'Yeah, the beginning.' He nodded his head, looked like he was trying to compose himself.

'Jonny, whatever it is, just tell me,' Freya spoke.

'My father was a labourer. You know that. He worked building sites. He earned OK money but he drank it away. My mother...well I never told you...she...she was a prostitute.'

'Oh, Jonny!'

'She did quite well for herself. I mean she started out on the streets, but then she managed to get herself a permanent place at the bar of one of the better hotels in that area of London. It paid OK, and when I was a kid I never wanted for anything. I always had new clothes and football boots and a bike. Then I met you.' He paused for breath.

Freya sat down on the other stool to listen to him.

'I thought you were the prettiest girl I'd ever seen. You were always smiling and laughing...always. I don't think I ever saw you without a smile on your face.' He smiled and looked over to her.

'I never smiled when I lost at bowling,' she reminded him.

'And that wasn't often as I remember.' Freya smiled.

'That night when you took me to meet Eric and Barbara, your parents, I remember thinking they weren't so bad. They were nice to me and we had Chinese takeaway. I thought I could do a lot worse than to have in-laws like them. I was so excited it had gone so well, I went home and told my parents about us. I told them who you were and who your parents were and how much I loved you and how we were going to get married,' he continued.

'I never knew.'

'Well, that's when it all went wrong. My mother was furious. I'd never seen her that angry before. She told me I was too young to get married. She said it was a ridiculous idea and I had to stop seeing you immediately.'

'What? Why?'

'That's what *I* said, but she wouldn't answer me. She and my father had a blazing row that night. They were both drunk, throwing stuff around and acting crazy. And this was all caused by me telling them about our relationship.'

'I don't understand.'

'No, neither did I. Until she took me to the hotel the next afternoon. Your father was there. I don't know which was worse, the look on his face or the expression I know was on mine.' He sucked in another breath and blew it out slowly. 'And my mother, she just turned to me and said…I'll never forget the words. She said *Jonathan, I think you met Eric last night, over Chinese. Well, love, he's your real father.*'

Freya stared at him, unable to take in what he was saying as he continued with the story.

'It turns out he was a client of hers, one of her regulars. Except that hadn't been enough for him. He had paid her a small fortune to have her exclusively and he had been having her for some years. I can only imagine what my conception was like.'

Freya just looked at him, her expression frozen.

'Anyway, what I'm trying to say is, Eric did wave his cheque book around back then, but not in the way you thought. He'd been paying monthly instalments to my mother ever since he got his DNA confirmation. He never saw me though, not once and he never even knew my name. In fact, the first time he set eyes on me, was over dinner with you, although he didn't know it at the time.' He put a shaking hand to his bottle of beer. 'So, after that afternoon in the hotel, he got my father a job on the other side of London and he paid for me to go to university. And that was that. I never saw him again until about five years ago.'

'Is this some sort of sick game of his? Has he paid you to come here and tell me this bullshit to freak me out?' She got down from the stool.

'No, it's the truth. Like it or not, you and I…we're half brother and sister. And that's why I had to leave. That's why we couldn't be together.'

Freya felt the nausea rise up in her throat and before she could stop herself she was vomiting into the sink. She wretched over and over and panic overwhelmed her.

Jonathan moved to help her. He gently touched her arm and Freya removed her head from the sink. She stepped away from him like she'd been hit by a bolt of lightning.

'Is everything OK in here?' Roger queried as he and Jolie entered the room.

'Yes, it's fine. Just leave us alone, please,' Jonathan spoke.

'Freya?' Roger asked.

'Actually, I don't feel so good. I feel a bit lightheaded and...' She couldn't control her breathing. Her heart was pounding and the room was spinning.

She heard the front door burst open. Nicholas entered the kitchen and she fell.

'Oh my God! You told her! You idiot! Roger, get an ambulance. Get an ambulance now!' Nicholas yelled.

'What's happened to her?' Jonathan questioned as Nicholas picked Freya up from the floor.

'Her blood pressure's been going up and she's been fainting. I wonder what could have brought *that* on?! Jolie, could you fetch a blanket? There are some in the cupboard at the top of the stairs.' He lifted Freya into his arms and made his way down the hall.

'Of course,' Jolie answered.

Nicholas lay Freya on the sofa and stroked her hair back from her face. Her skin was pale and moist with sweat.

'Come on, Freya. Just hold on for the ambulance. They won't be long, I promise.'

'Is she going to be alright?' Jonathan asked, entering the room.

'How should I know?! I'm not a doctor am I! But I tell you something, you'd better start praying she's going to be OK or you and daddy are going to wish you'd never set eyes on me.'

'Here's the blanket,' Jolie said. She tucked the throw around Freya.

'Thanks, Jolie. Sorry about this. Roger, where's the damn ambulance?' Nicholas called.

'I'm having trouble getting through,' Roger shouted in reply.

'Forget it! We'll take her. Get the keys to the SUV.' He picked Freya up again and made his way to the front door.

'Look, take my car. It's quicker than that thing and there's more room than your car,' Jonathan offered.

'I don't want anything to do with you,' Nicholas hissed.

'Don't be stupid, Nick. For God's sake, just take the car. Take it for Freya.' He held the keys out.

Nicholas grabbed the keys, Jolie opened the front door and they all went down the porch steps and onto the driveway.

'Do you want me to come with you?' Jolie asked, helping Nicholas settle Freya onto the back seat of the car.

'No, Jolie, you go home. Thanks for staying with Freya tonight. I…'

'Give me the keys. You get in the back with Freya. I'll drive,' Roger ordered.

'I'll wait here. Secure the house if you like,' Jonathan offered.

'Call yourself a cab. There's nothing valuable in the house. The only thing *I* care about is laid out on the back seat of the car.' Nicholas got in the car and slammed the door behind him.

Roger sped off up the driveway and out of the gate, just missing the half a dozen photographers camped outside.

Twenty Five

There's no place like home, there's no place like home, there's no place like home.

Freya was Dorothy. Jonathan was the cowardly lion. Nick was the tin man. Willis was Toto. Her father was the Wizard of Oz. And the Yellow Brick Road wasn't made out of bricks, it was made out of gold ingots and Freya wasn't seeking the wizard's advice. The cowardly lion was chasing her. He was telling her to stop and listen. Toto was weaving in and out of her legs trying to trip her up. The tin man, who she was trying to reach, seemed to be getting further and further away. The Wizard of Oz was laughing, over and over again and the noise was getting louder and louder until she couldn't hear herself think. She wanted to scream.

Freya snapped open her eyes, her breathing rapid, her face damp. Her head throbbed and her throat was sore. There was a familiar, eye ball penetrating, bright, white light above her head. It was then she knew she was in Carlton General Hospital again.

'Hi,' Nicholas whispered. He touched Freya's arm and leaned closer to her from his seated position at the side of her bed.

'Hi.'

'How are you feeling?'

'Was I shot or something? Because I feel like I've been shot…in the head.'

'No, no shooting. Just another collapse.' He stroked the hair off her face.

'I had a horrible, horrible dream.' She tried to sit up.

'Dr. Stone says you're to lie still. He'll be here soon. Tell me about the dream.'

'Well, it was kind of the *Wizard of Oz* but without the singing and dancing. And my father was the wizard, so I think I was doomed from the outset.' She gave half a smile.

'Freya, about what Jonny told you tonight…'

'Can you go and hurry up Dick Van Dyke? I'd really like to go home and finish the Ben & Jerry's I started,' she interrupted.

'He isn't lying about being your half-brother. It's the truth.'

'I can't believe he's fooled you. Who d'you think is behind all this? My father. And *my father* will pay anyone to say anything just to piss me off. This is all part of some elaborate master plan to make my life shit. Although he really didn't need to employ Jonny again. The dead birds were kind of freaking me out anyway.'

'Eric told me himself.'

Freya inhaled a breath and held it there.

'Going to see him was the right thing to do. It was the *only* thing to do.'

'You were going to keep it a secret from me. You lied to me about going to an interview! All those things we said about trust. All the guilt you made me feel about keeping my meeting with Jonny from you and days later you were lying to me about my father!'

'Freya, please, calm down.'

'No, I won't calm down. You know how I feel about that man. You know how dangerous he is and you didn't listen. And now he's playing you. Now he's created this ridiculous story about Jonny to hurt me and push us apart and you're falling for it.'

She began to pull at the drip, trying to disconnect herself.

'Freya, what are you doing? Don't be stupid. Come on, lie back down.'

'You've played right into his hands.' She started to untie her hospital gown.

'Freya, stop. Just stop and sit down. Just for a minute.' He grabbed her arm.

'I don't want to stop. I want to get out of this place.'

'I don't think your father's behind the break ins.'

'My God, he really took you right on in, didn't he? What did you expect him to say to you? *Yes, Nick it's me who's been terrorising you both. It was me who half-killed your driver and broke into your home.* Offer you brandy and cigars did he?'

'He as good as held his hands up about Mike. But I really don't think he's behind the other stuff.'

'And did you come to that conclusion before or after he told you this bullshit about Jonny being my half-brother?' She started to dress.

'Freya, I know you're upset but it doesn't really change anything for us. It doesn't change anything for you and me.'

'No of course it doesn't. Because it isn't true.'

'I don't see what your father had to gain by telling me if it wasn't the truth.'

'He's trying to mess with my head. That's what he does. I keep telling you that, Nick. Why don't you believe me?' She pulled her top over her head.

'It isn't that I don't believe you. I just think…'

'You just think what?' She stopped getting dressed and stared at him.

'I think you've got a lot on your mind at the moment.'

'And?'

'And I think you need a break. You need some time away. Time away from everything.'

'What I *need* is for everybody to get off my back and leave me alone.' She rushed to dress and then let out a breath and locked eyes with Nicholas.

'Look, I just want to get home. Can we go home? Can we talk about this later? Please,' she begged.

'I'd rather you saw the doctor first.'

'He probably isn't going to tell me anything you haven't told me already.'

'Why don't I go and speak to him? I'll see if he's happy for you to go. Then maybe we can call in tomorrow and he can check you over then.'

Freya nodded.

'OK, I won't be a minute.' He left the room.

She put her hands to her temples. Her head was bursting and she was still feeling panicked, but she wasn't going to admit that. She couldn't stand spending one more moment in the hospital.

A couple of minutes passed by and then Dr. Stone entered the room, closing the door behind him.

'Do I need to sign forms? Here, I have a pen.' She reached into her bag and produced a ballpoint.

'Freya, I think you know what I want to talk to you about.' His voice couldn't have been more serious.

'I feel fine. I'm a little tired, but fine, honestly.' She forced a smile.

'I'd really like you to have a scan. I'm becoming convinced your pregnancy might be contributing to the severity of your blood pressure and the fainting. We really need to check on the baby.'

'Can I go home please?'

'Freya, I'm afraid ignoring the issue isn't going to make it go away.'

'There's no issue to ignore.' She raised her eyes to meet Dr. Stone's.

'Then have the scan. Set my mind at rest.'

'No.'

'What are you afraid of?'

'Excuse me?'

'What are you afraid of?' the doctor repeated.

'I'm afraid that at any moment, Julie Andrews is going to appear and you're both going to re-enact a rooftop scene,' Freya answered.

'Freya, I don't think you realise the seriousness of the situation. Your baby could be in danger.'

'This is ridiculous. You can't keep me here, I'm leaving.' She got up and headed for the door.

'Then you leave me with no choice. I'm going to have to tell Nick.'

'Hello? Hippocratic Oath! Mean anything to you?'

'I will not allow you to put your child in danger, Hippocratic Oath or not. That would go against everything I believe in. And I really don't think you'd deliberately put your baby at risk.'

Freya didn't respond. She stood, frozen to the spot, her hand on the handle of the door.

'I realise this is all a bit of a shock to you but...' Dr. Stone began.

'Enough. I can't take any more of this emotional blackmail, it's out of order. I'll have the scan. Just get it done and get it done quickly so I can get out of here.'

'I'll arrange it now.'

He left the room and Freya stepped out behind him, joining Nicholas in the corridor.

'OK?' Nicholas asked, taking hold of her hand.

'Yes. Can we go now?' She watched Dr. Stone disappear up the corridor.

'Sure.'

Once outside, Freya filled her lungs with the cold, winter night air in attempt to clear her head of everything inside it. She really didn't know how much more she could take of life at the moment. Everything seemed to be falling apart.

'Roger drove us here but I sent him home. There was no point to him waiting around.' He pointed the electronic key fob at Jonathan's car.

'What's going on? Where's our car? This isn't our car.' She let go of Nicholas' hand and stopped.

'No, well, it was all a rush to get you to the hospital. The Ferrari wasn't practical, neither was the bike and your car isn't too streamlined. Jonny insisted we use his.'

'It was a rush to get me to the hospital so you debated which car you should drive? I can't go in this car.'

'I didn't want to use it, but it was the most practical thing to do.'

'I can't get into this car,' she repeated.

'Freya, I…'

'Aren't you listening to me?! I can't get in this car. It's his! It smells of him, and my father, and the money. It will make me feel sick and…I feel dirty. I feel so dirty.' It was then everything hit her. What if what

Jonathan said was true? How did she deal with that? She started to struggle for breath. Tears fell from her eyes.

'Hey, it's OK. It's OK.' He took her in his arms, cradling her body, enveloping it in his.

'He can't be my brother, he just can't be. I loved him. I loved him and we…we did things together and that's sick! *I'm* sick! What must you think of me?'

'None of this is *your* fault. None of it, Freya. I don't think anything.' He stroked her hair.

'My family's twisted, completely twisted. I can't have come from them, I can't have! I mean, if I'm going to find out anything else I'm begging I find out I'm adopted.' She swiped at her eyes with her fingers.

'I admit that would be good.'

'Why is this happening? Why is everything going wrong?'

'I don't know. You sure as hell don't deserve it.'

Freya took her head out of Nicholas' embrace and looked up at him, her eyes wet and her face tear-stained.

'Dr. Stone thinks I'm pregnant,' she blurted out.

'What?'

'I don't think I am. I mean we're careful and I'm not even sure he's a real doctor. I mean, he doesn't look like a doctor does he?' She watched Nicholas absorb what she'd told him.

'You're pregnant?' he repeated.

'I might be. But probably not. Because I would know, wouldn't I?'

'Well, how do we find out? Have you done a test?'

'No…I…well Dr. Stone wanted me to have a scan but there's no point. I mean I would know, wouldn't I?'

'Come on, we have to go back. We have to know,' Nicholas said, taking hold of her hand and pulling her towards the hospital entrance.

'But I can't be pregnant. I mean...'

'Freya, if you're pregnant this is absolutely the best news I've ever had.' A smile spread across his face.

'Really?' She still felt so uncertain.

'Why do you sound so surprised? We talked about how we felt about children when we first met,' Nicholas reminded her.

'Yes and do you remember what I said?'

'You said something about not being able to look after your houseplants.'

'Exactly.'

'Come on. Let's go and find out. What are you afraid of?' He squeezed her hand.

'That's what Dr. Stone asked me.'

'And what did you tell him?'

'I made some stupid comment about *Mary Poppins*,' Freya told him.

'Well, I'm sure he won't hold it against you. Come on, we could be on the verge of becoming parents.' There was thick excitement in his voice.

'On the verge of bringing a poor innocent child into this warped, twisted, creepy, weird circus of a life we live. Is it any wonder I'm terrified?'

'This will be a chink of light in the craziness though, wouldn't it?'

'It would mean we have a damn good case for suing Durex.'

'Freya, you could be having our baby. A baby I didn't really believe I would ever have...no matter what the doctors told me.' He let out a breath.

'I know.' She could see the expectation in his expression.

'So, let's go and see if we have something to celebrate. What have we got to lose?'

'Nine months of alcohol and all the dignity I ever had?'

'But eating for two. Come on, that has to interest you.'

'You're right,' she agreed with a nod. 'A valid excuse to eat takeaway for breakfast, lunch and dinner. Take me back.'

Nicholas smiled at her, leading the way back into the hospital.

Twenty Six

The alarm clock was showing 6.34am and Freya lay in bed, staring at the piece of paper in her hand. It was a small black and white picture of a grey blob. There was just a faint outline of four stumps attached to the blob. It was a picture of their baby. She was ten weeks pregnant.

She still found it impossible to believe. She knew the practicalities of how it got there but, even looking at it now, seeing what they'd both seen on the monitor at the hospital...it still didn't feel real. She was going to become a mother. That fact alone scared the hell out of her. The majority of the time she had trouble looking after herself. What was she going to do when she became responsible for someone else? And not just *someone else*, someone small and helpless. Someone who was going to look to her for everything. It was an enormous task and something she hadn't given full and proper consideration to at any time in her life before. Now, she only had just over six months to prepare herself.

She felt Nicholas stir and he turned over in the bed to face her.

'Hey,' he greeted.
'Morning.'

'Still looking at our baby?' He leaned up on his elbow and joined her gazing at the picture.

'Do you think its head's OK? It looks kind of square.' She held the photo closer to the bedside lamp.

'Then he or she must take after you. Have you never noticed your slight corners?'

'Not funny.'

'It looks perfect to me and Dr. Stone said everything was normal. The heartbeat was fine and that's all you can ask for at this stage.'

'I can't believe I have the responsibility of carrying it around for the next six and a half months.'

'I'll do you a deal. You carry it around for the next six and a half months and I will do more than my fair share for the next eighteen years or so.'

'You think I'm going to forget to feed it, like my houseplants.'

'No, I just want you to know that I'm all in. I want to be there for everything. The feeding, the diapers…you name it.'

'They're called nappies. Please call them nappies,' Freya begged.

'OK, nappies. So, how do you feel about it now? I mean in the cold, almost light, of day?'

'How do I feel about what? The baby? The fact my ex-fiancé is apparently my half-brother? Or the fact someone's breaking into our home and chopping me out of photographs?'

'How do you feel about the most important of those things?'

'Eric is a no-no for a boy's name. And Jane is definitely out for a girl's. I wouldn't want to give up work completely. But if we have a nanny I want to personally interview them all. Oh and I'm not breastfeeding.'

'I'm fine with all of that.' He leant forward and kissed her.

Freya put her arms around him, still holding the photograph. She held him close to her, breathing in the scent of him.

'Let's get married. Let's just go and do it,' she whispered.

'Not this again. We decided on a date, didn't we? This wonderful news doesn't change anything. We have six and a half months to make sure you're a Kaden before he or she is,' Nicholas reminded her.

'I'm not saying it because of the baby. I'm saying it because I don't want to wait a minute longer. I want to get married now, today. We can do that, can't we? There must be ways of arranging it.'

'If this isn't because of the baby, then this is because of Jonny.'

Freya stiffened at the mention of his name.

'I think maybe you should talk to him.'

'Talk to him?! Right now all I want to do is throttle him! All these years and not a word. All these years believing my father paid him off when, in fact, the truth was much worse! What we did was disgusting. Not to mention illegal and what if I'd got pregnant or something? What then? We could be talking eleven fingers and a face like the Elephant Man.' She got out of bed, grabbed her robe and wrapped it around her.

'Freya, you didn't know any of that at the time you were dating. He didn't know either. Now, I'm not the guy's greatest fan, but I'm guessing he must be feeling this too.'

'Don't have any sympathy for *him*! He's had over ten years to come to terms with this. I've had about ten hours! I don't think you can begin to understand how I feel.'

'Of course I can't. But I can tell you now, you can stop trying to take some of the blame. Like I told you last night, none of this is your fault. How could it be?'

'I don't want to see him ever again.'

'I think you two have issues you need to be discuss.'

'I think there are issues *you and I* have to discuss. Like how the hell are we going to stop people breaking into our home without getting one of those hideous twenty foot high fences. I mean, so much for motion sensors and security lighting. And if this isn't my father's work, then who's behind it?' She started to pace.

'Freya, sit down. Stress isn't good for the baby. Dr. Stone said…'

'Oh no, don't do this. I cannot put up with *Dr. Stone said this* and *Dr. Stone said that* for the next six months. And you can forget about wrapping me up in cotton wool because the over protective act doesn't do anything for me at the best of times. It certainly isn't going to cut it now.'

'Come on, Freya. It isn't wrong to want to protect you and our baby. I realise you're more than capable of looking after yourself but at least let me feel I'm needed.' He gave her a smile. One of his best ones. One of the ones that made her weak at the knees.

'I'll have a large pot of tea and some of the Jell-O stuff.'

'Fine, I'll go organise it.' He pulled back the covers and got out of bed.

Freya watched his naked form as he pulled on his underwear. She crossed the room fast and put her arms around his waist, holding his body close to her.

'Do you still think I'm sexy even now I'm incubating something?' she asked.

'Um, let me see. I think I'll have to remove that robe to really give an honest answer.' His fingers were at the knot, deftly unfastening it.

'I was kind of hoping you were going to say that.'

Twenty Seven

Freya and Nicholas finally got up just after eight thirty. Unable to wait any longer for breakfast, Willis had leapt up on the bed and paraded up and down the duvet until they had no choice but to give in.

While Nicholas made breakfast, Freya called Emma.

'Hello,' Emma answered.

'I'm ten weeks pregnant.'

'Oh my God! Freya! Ten weeks! Oh congratulations!'

'She's pleased,' Freya conveyed to Nicholas as Emma let out another shriek of excitement.

'What happened? Did you have the scan? What does Nick say?'

'Yes, I had the scan. I wasn't given any choice in the matter really. Dick Van Dyke was going on at me and then I kind of lost it in the car park about Jonny. Then I told Nick the doctor's suspicions and he took it all out of my hands. I think it was probably what I needed.'

'Whoa! Slow down, Freya. Jonny? Losing it in the car park? What's happened overnight?'

'More than you really want to know, believe me. It was definitely more than *I* wanted to know. I don't know where to start.'

'Just tell me,' Emma begged.

'Are you sitting down?'

She wasn't sure how she managed to get the words out. She'd rattled the news out as fast as she could to try and lessen the shock for her best friend. By the time Freya had stopped for breath both she and Emma were crying. Nicholas took the phone from her.

'Hi, Em,' he greeted, putting an arm around Freya and drawing her close.

'After what Freya's just told me, I feel like I need to come over and see her.'

'There won't be any need for that. We're planning on coming to Corfu straight after Freya's photography exhibition.'

'For a wedding?'

'We hope so.'

'Let me have her back,' Freya asked, reaching for the phone. Nicholas passed it to her.

'Sorry about that. I don't know what's the matter with me lately.' She wiped at her eyes.

'I can tell you exactly what's the matter with you, Freya. You have too much on your mind and you need a break. I don't know what to say about Jonny. I really don't, I mean...'

'I can't talk about him. Not yet, maybe not ever. It's too creepy and it turns my stomach and...' She felt nauseous again.

The buzz of the intercom interrupted their conversation. Freya paused to hear Nicholas answer and establish who it was.

'Hello,' Nicholas greeted.

'Nick? This is Harry, from *The Hollywood Chronicle*,' the voice replied.

'Harry, neither Freya or I have any comment to make on anything right now. I thought we had an arrangement with you. I thought that was one of the trade offs of Freya bringing you cups of tea in the morning for the last six months.'

'Oh I know. I don't want any comment on anything. I've just arrived here and someone's tied something to your gate. I just wanted to make you aware of it.'

'Emma, I'm going to have to call you back,' Freya said, ending the call.

'What is it, Harry?'

'Well, it's a wreath. And it's got Freya's name on it.'

'I'm coming down to the gate. Wait there and don't touch it.' He ended the conversation.

'A wreath with my name on. Well, fancy that.' She laughed but it came out weak.

'I'm going to call the police first and then I'm going to call Roger and we are getting CCTV out there today.' He pulled on a pair of sneakers.

'Wait, don't go yet. I want to see this for myself.' She picked up her jacket from the back of the chair and followed Nicholas down the hall.

The wreath was in the shape of a cross and it was made up of white carnations. Across it was a black ribbon with Freya's name printed on it and R.I.P written underneath.

'You haven't touched this have you, Harry?' Nicholas asked as he looked at the tribute.

'No. I called you as soon as I saw what it was.'

'And where are the others today? Has anyone been here before you? Has anyone photographed this?' Nicholas continued to question.

'I don't know. I think everyone's over at George Clooney's today. There were rumours he was making a big announcement this morning.'

Freya stared at the wreath. She read her name, looked at the perfectly white flowers and the contrast between the pretty blooms and the black ribbon.

'Just cut it down and put it in the bin,' she stated.

'I think we ought to let the police see it. They can check for fingerprints,' Nicholas told her.

'There won't be fingerprints. There were no fingerprints on the smashed windows, the crows or the "bitch" letter. This person's too clever to go handling things now.'

'You've been having people smash your windows?! I mean, I saw the police coming and going but…' Harry began.

'That's confidential, Harry. If it gets out I'll know who made the information public property. You get me?' Nicholas asked.

'Sure thing,' Harry replied.

Freya started to untie the wreath.

'Come on, let's go back inside.' He took the wreath from her and put an arm around her shoulders.

'Perhaps I should change the name and have it sent to Jonny,' she suggested as they walked.

'I think we should start thinking of anyone who might have a grudge against you besides your father.'

'Look, I know I can be a little abrasive, but making someone dislike me enough to do this sort of stuff? I can't think of anyone. Unless…'

'What? You've thought of someone?'

'Martha?'

'Martha?' Nicholas remarked.

'Yes, you can't have forgotten your old PA already! Stern suits, even sterner demeanour. The one you fired for being a complete bitch to me. She must despise me. I lost her her job.'

'I don't think this is Martha's thing. Anyway, she's working for Terry Quinlan now. I've heard she's having a ball bossing him around.'

'Well, you asked me to think of someone and that's the only person I can come up with. How about you? Can you think of anyone I've pissed off recently?'

'Not off the top of my head.'

'Then we're at a loss, aren't we? We'll just have to play a waiting game and hope we won't need to use this wreath for real.'

'Don't say that.'

'Oh my God,' Freya stated, clamping her hand to her mouth, her eyes widening.

'What?' Nicholas exclaimed as he pushed open the front door.

'Well, what event in my life did all this coincide with?'

'I don't know. You're going to have to elaborate.'

'It's Jonny. This all started after I met up with Jonny. That's who's behind it all. Not my father, but my father's clone.'

Twenty Eight

Freya arrived at Exposure ready to explode. On the drive in, all she could think about was Jonny and his potential involvement in this ugly business. Despite his pledge of support for the Every Day project, everything else in Freya's life had gone downhill since he'd reappeared on the scene. As much as she wanted her new found knowledge regarding their relationship to be erased from her memory banks, she now also wanted to know why he despised her so much and why he seemed to have turned into a carbon copy of their father.

'Morning, Sasha,' she greeted as she entered the reception area. She marched towards her office, barely giving her assistant a second glance.

'Oh, Freya, this is a surprise. I wasn't really expecting you in today. Wow! Your hair,' Sasha remarked, hurrying from behind the desk to follow Freya into her room.

'Weren't expecting me? Don't I have Miss Guide at eleven and Toby James at four?' Freya asked, looking down at her diary on her desk.

'Well, yes. But I wasn't sure, what with everything that's been going on, whether you'd feel up to working.'

'I feel fine. In fact, I feel better than ever. I mean, who wouldn't feel on top of the world when they have a gorgeous fiancé to marry in the next few weeks?' She smiled.

'I guess nobody.'

'Right, so, have you got my messages?'

'Um, yes. I'll just get them.' Sasha left Freya's office and headed back to the reception.

Freya began leafing through papers on her desk, looking for a Post-It note she knew she'd kept. She really needed to sort out the items on her desk. It was chaos and there was probably food under the files somewhere.

'Here you are. There are quite a few. I marked the ones I called back.' She passed Freya the message pad.

'Thanks, Sasha.' She took the book.

'So is everything OK at the house now? No more break ins or anything?' Sasha questioned.

'No, no everything's fine. In fact everything's more than fine.' She couldn't keep the smile from her face. Despite everything else that was going on, the baby news was wonderful. She might have reservations about her capabilities but she was excited. It was unexpected but not unwelcome.

'Really? You sound like you have some sort of news.'

'Well, actually I do. But it's completely confidential.'

She didn't want to share this news with the world. She'd hardly had time to take it all in herself yet. She wasn't ready to react to the world's reaction.

'That goes without saying.'

'Well, Nick and I…we're going to have a baby. Isn't that just the most exciting and terrifying news you've ever heard?'

'Wow. I mean, that's fantastic news, really great,' Sasha replied, smiling broadly.

'Yes it is, isn't it? I mean, I wasn't sure at first but Nick is so excited. And I think he's going to be a wonderful father.' She recalled his expression when he saw the image on the scan monitor the night before.

'I'm sure he will be amazing.'

'The only down side to the pregnancy is I seem to have totally gone off all the foods I used to crave. For example, the thought of eating leftover Chinese for breakfast makes me feel quite sick.'

'I'm sure it will pass.'

'I hope so. Because I can't see the baby getting all it needs from Jell-O sandwiches.'

'Would you like me to get you something from the patisserie?'

'No thanks. But a cup of tea would be great.'

'I'll go and make one.'

Miss Guide was one of the largest lingerie companies in the US and Freya knew her intimate photos of Nicholas were the reason she'd been asked to shoot for them. Although scantily-clad women were not her subject of choice, the job paid extremely well and Freya had also been able to suggest the company thought about making a range for the larger woman. They had taken this on board and Freya had agreed to endorse the product. She'd devoted the morning to looking at designs and trying on some prototypes. In between changes of underwear she'd telephoned Jonathan.

She'd got through to his voicemail and had left a message for him to meet her at Gatebrook.

It was just after one when Freya arrived and Jonathan was already there. He was stood, leant against the bonnet of his car, a pair of sunglasses in his hand. He looked more composed than the evening before. He was wearing a fresh suit and everything about him was immaculate and restored.

Freya pulled up in front of his car. Her stomach was churning. She didn't really know what to say to him. Taking a deep breath she got out and shut the door firmly behind her.

'Got your car back then,' she remarked. She walked towards him.

'Yeah, I went to the hospital last night but they said you'd already gone and I didn't want to call the house. I guessed, as you'd left, it meant things must be alright.'

'Things aren't alright, Jonny. Things are far from alright.' She threw the wreath at him. It landed on the bonnet of his car. Some of the flowers detached and fell to the ground.

'What is this?' he asked, looking at it.

'Oscar worthy! Come on, keep it up. Show me some real surprise and outrage. Nick says it's all in the stance. So, come on, Jonny, give me a stance.'

'Who sent you this?' he asked, moving his gaze from the flowers to Freya.

'Fantastic! Great line and perfectly timed. I wish I was recording this. Perhaps Nick could swing a part for you.'

'Freya, I don't know what you're talking about. Am I supposed to know what this is?' Jonathan questioned.

'The camera would love you. Hold on, I have Donald in my bag somewhere. Let me get some stills.' She dug into her handbag and looked for her camera.

'Freya, stop it. I don't know anything about this. Where did it come from? Was it sent to you? Have you informed the police? Stuff like this is serious intimidation.'

'It was tied to my front gate this morning for everyone to see, including some of the press. Well, *one* of the press. Apparently we're not as hot as George Clooney today.' She couldn't find the camera.

'And you think *I* had something to do with it? Why?'

'Now let me think! When did I start getting hate mail? Hmm, just after you reappeared. When did my beautiful house start getting broken into? Hmm, just after I met up with you again. When did our driver get attacked? Oh, let me fill in the blanks for you! When I started seeing you again!' she ranted.

'For God's sake, Freya. Why would I be doing this to you? I care about you.'

'Oh no. Don't you say that. Don't you say you care about me! If you cared about me you would not have told me what you told me. You would not have got in touch with me again to tell me that...'

'To tell you I'm your brother?'

'Stop it. Don't say that. I don't want to hear it.' She clamped her hands over her ears. The words still sickened her.

'You have to hear it. Take your hands away and bloody listen to me,' he ordered. He wrenched her hands away from her head.

'Let go of me! Don't you touch me! You make me feel sick.' Her heart was racing and she was starting to feel woozy.

'And how do you think I've felt about it since I found out? I've had to carry this around with me every day since I was seventeen. Our father bought my family's silence and we never spoke about it again. There were so many times I wanted to get in touch with you, to try and make sense of it all but I couldn't cross him.'

'You couldn't cross him because he was dipping into his pockets and providing you with everything you needed to become a cardboard cut-out of him.'

'What was I supposed to do? You know what my life was like on that council estate. I had no prospects. My future would either have been working my guts out in a factory like my father or pedaling amphetamines.'

'It didn't have to be that way. And there's nothing wrong with working hard for a living.'

'No, I agree, but struggling? Struggling to survive like my parents did for so many years? Letting my mother carry on selling herself just to put food on the table? Listening to her cry at night? Eric offered us all a lifeline and I'm sorry if that grates on you, but we took it.'

'He bought you. Just like he buys everything in his life. You're just another one of his possessions and he will use you and manipulate you forever.'

'I don't think he will.'

'Believe me, I'm speaking from vast experience.'

'This is going to sound really hard to believe, but…he cares about me.'

'Oh my God! You're kidding me, right? You think he cares about you! I didn't realise you were so naïve. The only person Eric Lawson-Peck cares about is himself and the only other thing he cares about is his fortune.'

'He's aging, Freya. He's nearly sixty years old and I think he's taking some time to reflect on things.'

'I can't stand here and listen to this crap. My father will never change. He's always been a piece of work and being eligible for his bus pass is not going to alter that.' She turned away from him and made her way back to the car.

'He's left me everything in his will.'

'Oh my! He's not left it to me? How shocked and surprised I am. How hurt and insulted. I'm pleased for you, Jonny. It sounds like you completely deserve it, having been so close to the man for all these years.'

'The money doesn't interest me. In ten or so years time, I plan to be worth twice as much as him.'

'Bravo.' She opened the door of her car.

'I want *you* to have the money. As soon as I inherit, I'm gifting it to you.'

'I can't be bought, you know that. I've no interest in the money either but for much better reasons than you. Like the fact taking anything from you or that man would be like selling my soul to the Devil.'

'Are you saying the Every Day project or the Nicholas Kaden Foundation could do without a few billion dollars?'

'It's dirty money, Jonny. Anything my father's associated himself with is soiled and that includes you.' Her eyes flashed at him, shooting anger across the yards.

'I never stopped loving you, Freya.'

'Don't you understand how that sounds? Whatever we felt for each other back then was wrong and disgusting. I have memories in my head that keep replaying and I don't ever want to see them again.'

'We did nothing wrong, Freya. We didn't know.'

'That doesn't make it alright. God, what sort of freak am I? My mother sleeps with my boyfriend and now I've slept with my half-brother. Anymore and they could probably dedicate a whole episode of *Jerry Springer* to me.'

'So, where do we go from here?'

'Where do we go from here? Well, I suggest you go that way and I'll go in the opposite direction. You didn't expect us to get together and all be one big happy family did you?'

'I didn't expect anything, but would that be such a bad thing?'

'You're serious, aren't you? You think you and I and *our* father can put our differences aside and let bygones be bygones! Jonny, you're completely insane. I can hardly bear to look at you.'

'I never had any siblings growing up.'

'Well, go back to Daddy. Ask him how many other prostitutes he slept with. There might be a whole new multi-cultural family waiting out there for you. We might even have to expand Friends Reunited to fit us all on there.'

'Can you blame me for wanting to be part of your life? We've missed out on so much.'

'Jonny, perhaps I'm not being plain enough. Stop sending me letters. Stop breaking into my house and ruining perfectly good photos of Nick and I. And stop with the floral tributes. I don't want your money. I don't want your help with the Every Day project and I don't want to see you again. For all I care you can go ahead and build a giant Recuperation Inn on this very spot.' She'd yelled so loud her throat hurt and tears were pricking her eyes.

'I never meant to hurt you.'

'Then you didn't try very hard.' She got into the car and slammed the door shut. Her fingers shook as she turned the key. She performed a u-turn, leaving Jonathan in her dust.

She trembled as she drove, her emotions overloaded. Her eyes brimmed with tears and she wiped at them with the back of her hand. All the good times she had with Jonathan, all the memories they'd shared together and the love they'd felt for each other had been destroyed. Recalling their time together would never be the same now their relationship had changed so drastically. All Freya felt now was hurt and disappointment of the severest kind. The foundations of her life had been built upon lies and deception and here she was, preparing for motherhood. She knew all the things she wanted to teach her child, things she had to learn for herself through trial and experience. But would she really be able to do it when so much of her world had been based on untruths?

    She needed to stop thinking about it so much. She needed to get absorbed in something else. She turned off the main road and headed for County Bridge.

Twenty Nine

At Whitewood House, Nicholas sat in the study trying to read through the same script. Ordinarily, he'd be reading outside but the weather had worsened. The sky was filled with grey clouds that threatened snow and there was a biting wind that chilled you to the bone. He took off his glasses and laid them on the desk, rubbing at his eyes. All he could hear was banging and drilling as the security team installed cameras and more equipment to secure the house. He wasn't getting very far and the lines had to be learnt before his trip to Africa.

There was a knock on the door.

'Yeah, Roger, come in.' He put the script to one side and swigging back the remains of his cup of tea.

Roger entered.

'Sorry to bother you. Sasha's here.'

'Hey, Sasha. Come on in,' Nicholas invited as she stepped forward and Roger ducked back out. 'Would you like a drink?'

'Oh, well I don't want to disturb you if you're busy. I just thought while Freya is out, I'd drop some things round here to surprise her.' She shook a pair of shopping bags at him.

'I'm about done. I can't seem to concentrate with all the noise going on. Would you like some tea?'

'Well, maybe a quick one. I want to get back to the office before Freya does though. Don't want her to think I'm slacking off.' She checked her watch.

'I'll make it quick. Hey, Roger! You and the guys want tea?' Nicholas called up the stairs.

'No thanks, Nick. We're all good up here.'

'You make everyone tea?' Sasha exclaimed.

They both moved into the kitchen and Sasha placed her bags on the breakfast bar.

'Yeah, sure. Why do you sound surprised? You've been here before. We don't have a team of butlers hiding in the closet, you know.' He laughed.

'I know. I just...I don't know. I mean, you're so famous and...' Sasha began, blushing.

'Don't say that to Freya. She hates the word "famous", only second to the word "celebrity",' Nicholas replied as he switched the kettle on.

'She told me about the baby. Congratulations.' She reached into one of the bags and pulled out a white all-in-one baby outfit.

"Oh, she told you. Well, we're just trying to keep it quiet right now. You know what the press is like. And it's early days so we don't want to tempt fate.'

'Do you like the outfit? I got some in white and lemon.' She rifled through the bags, pulling outfits out and holding them up.

'Sasha, they're great. You shouldn't have.'

'Well, I wanted to. What with everything that's been happening to you two, I thought you both deserved a treat. It must be terrible having someone come into your house. And then for someone to send a wreath. Freya must be out of her mind with worry.' She sat down on one of the stools.

'Well, I can't say it isn't unsettling. But Freya's coping really well. She's made of strong stuff and we're taking all the precautions we can. We're having a new electric fence installed today and there's two plain-clothes officers keeping an eye on the house.'

'How awful. I mean Mayleaf's such a lovely little town. You wouldn't think this sort of thing would happen here.'

'There are a lot of sick people out there. When you're in the public eye it's always a risk. I just never thought someone would do this to Freya.' He poured the water into the teapot.

'Why d'you think they're targeting Freya?'

'I have absolutely no idea. If I did I'd be helping the police catch whoever it is.'

'Maybe whoever it is is jealous of her,' Sasha suggested.

'Jealous? What makes you say that?'

'Well, who wouldn't be jealous of a woman with everything? She has a successful business and a fabulous home. She's admired by millions of people and she's about to get married to a handsome, Hollywood actor who some people would kill to be with.'

'Freya would probably say the successful business she built up through hard work. She'd say the fabulous home would be more fabulous if it didn't have so many bolts and sensors on it. The admiration she hates and as for the actor. Well, he's just an ordinary guy who moans when he doesn't have a clean shirt to wear and snores at night when he's had too much to drink.' He laughed and passed Sasha a cup.

She smiled and accepted it.

'Freya has an idea who's behind it.'

'She does? Someone she knows?'

'Someone she *thought* she knew, put it that way.'

'How awful. Is it someone from Mayleaf?'

'No, not from Mayleaf. God, the people in this town have been so supportive to us. Jolie from the store has been over here most days to see if we need anything. And Bruce from the Chinese has started sending over food parcels.'

'It's nice to have the community rallying around.'

'Yes it is. It's really important to me, especially now because I'm going to Africa in a few weeks time. I'd hate for Freya to be on her own. Mind you, considering what's been happening and with the baby on the way, I might not be able to leave her on her own.'

'How are the wedding plans coming along? I suspect with all the disruption you haven't been able to do much organisation.'

'Well, it's certainly been hectic. But who knows? We might manage it.' He smiled.

'Still planned for December twenty-second?'

'At the moment.'

'Good. I've ordered a little gift, you see.'

'Oh, Sasha, you really shouldn't have. And all these clothes are great. Thank you.'

'You're welcome. Well, I'd better go. I don't want Freya to find me missing.' She checked her watch.

'But you haven't finished your tea,' Nicholas remarked, looking at her full cup.

'No. Well, I don't want Freya to miss me and I left the answer phone on. I'd really better get back.' She stood up and headed towards the hall.

'Well, thanks for coming by and thank you again for the baby clothes. It's really generous of you and I'm sure Freya will appreciate it.' He followed her down the hall and opened the front door.

'I hope so.' She smiled.

'I'll see you.'

'Yes. See you soon.' She smiled again and stepped out onto the deck.

Thirty

When Freya arrived back home there were a dozen photographers outside. As soon as she brought the car to a halt they began surrounding it. The remote sensor to open the gate failed to work, so Freya had no choice but to get out of the vehicle and press the intercom.

'Freya, congratulations on your pregnancy. When's the baby due?' one of the reporters questioned.

A flash from a camera went off in Freya's face.

'It could arrive at any minute if you don't stop pushing me.'

She hoped Nicholas was in. She was going to look seriously stupid if she had to climb the fence into her own house. And she would probably get fried if Roger had installed the electric barbed wire.

'Hello.' Nicholas' voice came through the intercom.

'Nick, it's me. The bloody gate won't open and I'm being mauled by reporters. What happened to them being all over George Clooney today? Can you let me in before I'm savaged?'

'I think the security guys are updating the system. OK, you're in.'

The gate began to open and Freya hurried back to the car.

'Will the news of your pregnancy alter your wedding plans?' another reporter called as Freya got up into the SUV.

'Aren't you getting this? I don't have anything to say to you guys. Are you new?' Freya questioned, staring at one of the photographers.

'Me?' he inquired, lowering the camera briefly.

'Yeah, you. I haven't seen you before. And, by the way, you're holding that camera all wrong.'

With that comment made, Freya drove through the gate and up to the house.

She hurried up the steps and up to the front door, her key ready for the lock. She stopped. She stared at the door and saw the lock was gone and in its place was a keypad. She let out a frustrated sigh and just stared at the buttons, not knowing what to do.

Before she had a chance to take any further action Nicholas opened the door.

'Nick, what the hell is going on? There's a key pad where the lock used to be and the whole world knows I'm pregnant!"

'What?!'

'There are a dozen reporters, if not more, at the damn gate bombarding me with questions about the baby. I want to know how they know, because I've only told two people about this. One of them I trust implicitly and the other has her job to lose if I find out she's blabbed,' Freya blurted out as she moved past Nicholas into the house.

He stepped out onto the porch and looked down the driveway at the journalists congregated outside. Seeing enough, he stepped back into the house and shut the front door.

'What's going on? Oh my God, someone's erected a prison wall in the back of the garden.'

Looking through the patio doors leading from the kitchen into the garden, she could see a large metal fence surrounding the entire boundary.

'It isn't as bad as it seems. You'll get used to it. It's for our protection. And our protection is the most important thing.'

'I can't live like this.'

'I know.'

'I mean I really can't live like this. We discussed it, when I moved here. We said we were going to have a normal life, doing normal things, just *being* normal and you promised. You promised no electric fences, no cameras, no motion sensors.'

'I know.'

'Well what the hell happened? Look at this place! You can't move for security paraphernalia! I'm scared to breathe too heavy in case I set off an alarm and Willis hates it. Have you noticed he's spending more and more time outdoors? In *this* weather! They're expecting snow, you know!'

'I know all this, Freya. D'you think I'm enjoying living under lock and key? But you heard what the police said. We have to take every precaution, we'd be stupid not to. And now it's more important than ever. We have a baby to consider.'

'Oh my God, that's it! That is it! Enough! I've had enough!' Freya yelled, waving her hands in the air.

She turned on her heel, left the kitchen and headed for the stairs.

'Freya, come back.' He followed her.

'No. This last week has been just about the worst time of my entire life. And here was I thinking nothing could possible top my prison stay or my life in the

Lawson-Peck household,' Freya spat as she marched up the stairs and into their bedroom.

'It hasn't been all bad. We've made plans for our wedding and we've found out we're going to have a baby.'

'I've been sent a "bitch" letter and a wreath. We've had to open an account at the glaziers and the security firm. Our driver has been assaulted. We've been beating off dead crows on an almost daily basis. And, if that wasn't enough, I've just found out my ex-fiancé is actually my half-brother! Tell me those aren't good, strong, valid reasons to be pissed off?!' She tugged her suitcase off the top of the wardrobe.

'Of course they are. And I can't say I'm too thrilled about any of it either but…what are you doing with that suitcase?'

'What does it look like I'm doing? I'm packing.' She put the case down on the bed and opened it up. Then she pulled open a drawer and chucked in some tops.

'Oh no. No, you're not running away.'

'I need to get out of this completely crazy messed up life I have right now. I need to be somewhere else.' She opened another drawer and pulled out some trousers.

'You can't just leave. We've made plans and…' Nicholas started.

'I don't care. I can't stay here, Nick. It's making me ill. I can't look at another reporter. I don't want to see my face and news about our baby on the front of another magazine and I don't want to wait and see what my warped admirer has in store for me next.'

'Freya, this is stupid. Where are you going to go?'

'Where I always go.' She slammed the case shut and let out a sigh.

'Corfu.'

'Right on the money.' She picked the case off the bed.

'Fine. Well, give me two minutes. I'll pack some things and come with you,' Nicholas said. He went to the wardrobe and took down another suitcase.

'You want to come with me?'

'Well, you can't think I'm going to sit in this secure compound on my own.' He smiled at her.

'Fine. But you'd better hurry up because I want to be gone before the reporters out front start guessing the baby's weight already.'

'Understood. Packing only the essentials. Passport and underwear.'

'You've not run away before. Underwear is never an essential. Don't pack anything you wouldn't be able to sell, eat or turn into a lifejacket.' She walked towards the bedroom door.

'Fine. Hey! We'll need someone to feed Willis while we're gone.'

'I'll go and ask Jolie right now. Anything you want from the store while I'm there?'

'Something I can turn into a lifejacket?'

'Stop this! I'm the funny one. You're the straight guy,' Freya called back.

Thirty One

With the paparazzi unable to enter the Town Circle, Freya could walk around Mayleaf without fear of being followed and photographed. Despite the freezing conditions it was still a picture-perfect place. The trees were bare, there was frost on the branches and everyone she passed was bundled up in hats and gloves. She loved the town. It made her feel warm inside just walking the streets. It felt like home. She only hoped the security they were living under wouldn't last forever.

Sam and Jolie's store was quiet when Freya entered. That gave her unrivalled access to what she called "travelling food". It wasn't unusual for Freya to pack few clothes when escaping at the spur of the moment. But she rarely left without a family-sized bag of crisps and a huge chocolate bar.

'Look after Willis? I'd be delighted. Oh, I wouldn't have to set any difficult alarms or anything would I? I mean...' Jolie began.

'To be honest, Jolie, right now I couldn't care less if the place burnt down.' She picked up half a dozen chocolate bars from the counter.

'Oh no, you don't mean that do you? You love that house.'

'I *did* love it. When it didn't resemble Fort Knox.'

'Things no better? Haven't the police found who's responsible yet?' Jolie inquired.

'No, but then I'm sure they have far more important things to do, don't you?'

'So, how long are you going to be away for?'

'I don't know yet. A week? Maybe two? Don't worry, Willis has stacks of food. And if he does go through it all, just get whatever he needs and charge it to our tab.'

'No problem. And don't you worry about anything. You both deserve a break. Make sure you enjoy it. By the way, have I heard right? Are you two hearing the patter of tiny feet?' Jolie asked, a broad smile on her face.

'What?'

'Are you having a baby? I don't usually believe what I hear on some of those news channels, but I've had five or six customers asking me about it this afternoon and…' Jolie began.

'It's true, we're going to be parents. We were trying to keep it under wraps but that seems impossible in our lives.' She let out a sigh and grabbed another two chocolate bars.

'Well, I think it's wonderful news. You two are going to make great parents.' She moved from behind the counter to put her arms around Freya and hug her.

'I'll be needing all the advice I can get. Particularly on the whole getting it out of my body stuff, because I'm really no good with pain.'

'You'll be fine.'

'I was fine with the getting it in there thing. I enjoyed that, a lot. I suppose what goes up must come down, one way or another. Perhaps I should abuse my privileged status and demand a C-section.'

'I think you'll find they're not all they're cracked up to be. My sister could tell you a thing or two about them.'

'Please don't give me her number.' Her mobile phone began to ring.

'It's Nick...hello.'

'Hey, could you pick up some bottled water? We're all out.'

'I will. I'm nearly done here.' She smiled at Josie and picked up the brown grocery bag.

'OK, well everything's ready to go. Roger's going to take us to the airport and I've arranged flights. We leave in a couple hours.'

'I can't wait to be on that island. I can't wait to be away from alarm systems.' She waved at Josie, left the store and headed for her car.

'No, me neither. It'll be good to see Emma and Yiannis again. Oh, I forgot to tell you. Sasha called around earlier. She bought some baby clothes. She wanted to drop them off to surprise you. I put them in the guest room for now.'

'Sasha? Well, what was she doing out of the office? She was supposed to be meeting with someone at two. What time was this?' She opened the car door and put the groceries on the passenger seat before hopping up into the driver's side.

'Come on, Freya. Get out of Boss Lady mode. It was a nice thing for her to do. She said after you finding the wreath and stuff she wanted to do something to cheer you up.'

'She said what?' She exhaled and felt a chill run up her.

'She said after a shock like getting sent a wreath with your name on, you needed something to take your mind off of it.'

'Nick, I didn't tell Sasha about the wreath.'

'Well, she knew about it. I bet you, despite what Harry promised us, he's been spreading that information around.'

'Have you heard it reported? Did any of the press at our gate ask you about it? Have the police released any details about it? Because no one's said a word to me about it. But they've all been more than keen to ask me about the baby.' Her mind was working overtime. She was certain she hadn't mentioned the wreath to Sasha. It could only mean one thing but that couldn't be true.

'What are you saying?' Nicholas asked her.

'I think you've said enough to him, don't you?' Sasha spat.

Freya felt something press in to the back of her head and she held her breath. She flicked her eyes up to the rear view mirror and saw Sasha sat in the back seat of the car. The hard object at the back of her head was the barrel of a gun.

'Nick, it's her! It's Sasha!' Freya shrieked at the top of her voice.

'Freya? Freya, are you there?'

Sasha snatched the phone from Freya's hand and ended the call.

'Stupid, stupid Freya! Always such a big mouth and never knows when to keep it shut!' Sasha yelled.

The gun pressed harder into Freya's head and she winced.

'Now, are we going to be adult about this or not? Are you going to behave or am I going to have to make this even more unpleasant for you?' Sasha hissed, her mouth close to Freya's ear.

Freya's heart was racing and her head began to swim. She couldn't faint now. She had to remain in control.

'Didn't you hear me?! I said, are you going to behave?' The gun stabbed into her skull.

'Yes. Yes, please don't hurt me.' She held in a whimper that was threatening to slip from her lips.

'*Ooo please Sasha, don't hurt me!* You sound so pathetic.' Sasha climbed over into the passenger seat, dropping the grocery bag to the floor.

Freya made a grab for the handle of the door. Sasha immediately locked all the doors.

'Didn't you hear what I said, bitch? Anymore stupid moves and I'll finish this here and now.' Sasha grabbed Freya's arm and squeezed it hard.

Freya fought back the tears and just stared at Sasha. The woman's face was a picture of rage and hate and almost unrecognisable from that of the helpful, dutiful assistant she worked with every day.

'Right, I want you to drive. I'll give directions. Start the car,' Sasha ordered, keeping the gun trained on Freya.

'Where are we going?' With shaking hands she turned the key in the ignition.

'You'll know when we get there. Take a right at the junction.'

Suddenly there was a knock on the driver's side window. Freya jumped as she saw Brian's face looking in at her.

'Wind down the window and talk to him. Tell him everything's fine, then get rid of him.' Sasha concealed her weapon.

Freya did as she was told and fixed a smile on her face as she greeted her neighbour. She turned the ignition off.

'Hi, Brian.'

'Hello, Freya. I saw you parked here and I thought I'd take this opportunity to ask you about a merchandising idea I have.'

'Merchandising? Well...I...perhaps you'd better talk to Nick about that. He's more into that sort of area. He's at the house if you wanted to go there and see him. Tell him I sent you.' She winked heavily, hoping he would realise something was wrong.

'Well, you know Mayleaf has a baseball team - the Mayleaf Maulers - well I thought to drum up support and in recognition of the team reaching the quarter finals of the county league, I could print some t-shirts.'

'T-shirts.' She looked past Brian towards the store, in the hope Sam or Jolie would come out.

'Yes, I was hoping you'd agree to the slogan "Baby Kaden says Go Maulers Go". I mean obviously he/she/it wouldn't actually say that, but I'd like to think one day he/she/it might join the team and...' Brian carried on.

'You know what, Brian, I think it's a great idea. I really think you should speak to Nick about it and...' Her eyes pleaded for Brian to come out of his world and join hers. It wasn't happening.

'Hey, Freya, hadn't we better get going? We don't want to be late for that appointment,' Sasha spoke loudly, leaning over Freya and smiling at Brian.

'Yes. Yes, we'd better get going. Brian, why don't you go up to the house and...' Freya began again.

'Bye, Brian,' Sasha interrupted. She closed the window up.

Brian smiled and waved.

'Simpleton. How unlucky are you, Freya? Someone comes right up to the car when you're being held at gunpoint and of all the people it has to be him. And he asks you about t-shirts,' Sasha laughed.

'Look, what the hell is all this about? Why are you doing this?'

'Shut the fuck up and drive! No more small talk.' Sasha poked the gun into Freya's cheek.

She had no choice. She re-started the car.

Thirty Two

'Shall we have some music? I think I'd kind of like some music right now. What have we got in here? Urgh, Aerosmith. How very rock chick of you.' Sasha began to flick her way through the CD collection.

'Actually that one's Nick's.'

'Is it? One of his favourites? Now that's something I didn't know about him. An admiration of Steve Tyler. Well, I suppose I could live with that.' She pushed the disc into the player.

'I don't understand this, Sasha. When did you start hating me so much?'

'When did I start hating you? Hmm, let me think about that. Well, I think it was probably about the time you started dating my guy.'

'What?'

'Nick's my guy, you know. He doesn't really know it yet, but it's only a matter of time.' She nodded her head to the beat of the music.

'You've got a crush on Nick? *That's* what all this is about?'

'I don't have a *crush* on him. I'm not some sort of deluded teenager. I'm in love with him. And, if it wasn't for you pushing yourself on to him, he'd be in love with me,' Sasha informed her.

'This is very bizarre. I mean I've liked guys before, all sorts of guys and believe me I've been let down by more than a few. But I've never felt the need to take a gun to someone's head.'

'Aren't you listening to me you stupid, fat bitch? I'm in love with him! Don't you know what that means? It means that he's going to be mine and you are surplus to requirements. You *and* that brat.' Sasha let out a scream of hysteria and aimed the gun at Freya's stomach.

Freya swallowed and tried to remain focused on the road ahead.

'This wasn't how it was supposed to end up, you know. It was supposed to go on a lot longer than this, but you had to ruin that for me too. Making plans to get married and this afternoon, trying to jet off to Corfu,' Sasha remarked, tapping the gun on the dashboard in time to the music.

'How can you possibly know about Corfu? We only decided that half an hour ago.'

'I know everything, Freya! I admit things got a little patchy when you lost your handbag, but I still had the wire in the house. I know absolutely everything you and Nick have discussed over the last few months.'

'My God.'

'Now, perhaps you'll have a little respect for me, instead of treating me like someone with no brain. *I'll have a cup of tea please, Sasha. I'll have another calorie loaded pastry, Sasha,*' Sasha spoke.

'That isn't how it is at all. I've been nothing but nice to you. I gave you the job even though you were the least qualified for it. I've told you things I know about photography I haven't passed on to anyone else. I thought we were friends.'

'I know you did. That was the plan. You had to trust me for any of this to work.'

'I still don't really understand why you've been doing all this. Was it *all* you? The broken windows? The photographs? The letter and the wreath? What about Mike? Did you arrange for him to be attacked?' Freya wanted to know.

'I'd like to say that it was all me, but no. I had nothing to do with poor Mike's attack. That hurt Nick, didn't it? He treats all his staff well, just like friends. I saw how that affected him. I couldn't do anything that would hurt him,' Sasha replied.

'You couldn't do anything to hurt him?! What d'you think all this has been doing to him? He's been worried out of his mind. He loves me, Sasha.'

'Shut up! He does *not* love you! He's just got confused. *You've* made him confused. You turned up in his life when he was vulnerable over his cancer. He was an easy target and you manipulated him into a relationship with you. The poor guy didn't stand a chance. But I'm going to save him from that.'

She was sounding unhinged. Nothing like the person Freya thought she had got to know over the past few months.

'Look, Sasha, I know how you must feel...'

'Know how I feel?! You have absolutely no idea how I feel! Do you know how sick I've felt having to work with you every day? I've had to listen to all that boring camera talk in the office and watch you fawning all over Nick. And as for listening to the two of you at home...the sex actually turned my stomach. I pity Nick, having to put up a pretence of enjoying himself. It just shows what a fantastic actor he is.'

'You're twisted,' Freya said through gritted teeth.

'Like *you're* one to judge! I heard the conversation with your "brother". I have to say that gave me great amusement. I listened to him telling you, you completely freaking out, so much so you had to go to hospital! Imagine! Sleeping with your brother! Now, *that* is twisted.' She laughed.

Anger boiled up inside Freya and she pulled hard right on the steering wheel of the car. The SUV veered across the road towards the embankment. It hit the bank and came to a halt.

'You stupid bitch! Get out the seat! Get out the seat. You're getting in the back,' Sasha screamed, pointing the gun at Freya.

'Whatever you have planned for me doesn't really matter. Nick will be on his way here with the police and you're going down for kidnap, harassment and breaking and entering at the very least.'

'And, pleading insanity, how long do you think I will get? You *are* the sentence expert after all.' Sasha pushed Freya into the back seat of the car.

'Whatever you get, you won't be getting Nick.'

'Hmm, you don't think? With you not here, with him needing support and a shoulder to cry on…with me explaining what I did, I did for us? I can picture it all now. Nick, me and our future.'

'You're seriously deluded.'

'Don't forget, Freya, I'm the one with the gun. So I'd think twice before making any more comments. Now, put your hands behind your back.' Sasha pulled a roll of twine out of her bag.

'This is pointless, you know. I really don't see what you're going to achieve,' Freya continued as Sasha began to tie her hands together behind her back.

'I told you. I'm going to get rid of you. I'm doing this for Nick as much as for me.' She pulled the wire tight around Freya's hands.

'You keep telling yourself that.'

'You can't really think he's in love with you! Look at you for God's sake! What would he see in an oversized frump like you?' She took Freya's face in her hands and squeezed her cheeks.

'You can do what you like to me. But just think about what you'll be doing to Nick's baby.'

Sasha's nails dug into her flesh and Freya could feel her breath on her face.

'Do you really think I give a damn about that? It's just another obstacle in the way that'll be removed. In fact it will be killing two birds with one stone. And how appropriate that is.' A smug smile spread across Sasha's face.

'You might have heard everything we've done over the last few months, Sasha. But you won't have seen Nick's face when he saw our baby on the monitor at the hospital. He was overjoyed. There were tears in his eyes and he looked at the image as if it were the most amazing thing he'd ever seen. To him it was only one stop short of a miracle.'

'Oh quit with the dramatics. It's just a baby. I can give him a baby. *I* can give him a baby *and* get my figure back afterwards. I don't hold out much hope for you.' She jabbed Freya in the stomach with the gun.

'What sort of person are you? Don't you care about anything except this ridiculous obsession with my fiancé?' Freya wanted to know.

Sasha slapped Freya's face. The force of the blow had Freya reeling back into the seat.

'He is *not* your fiancé. Not anymore. Now, I don't want to hear another word from you or I'll end this right here…right now.'

Freya sat still on the seat, unable to move with her hands tied behind her back. She watched, helpless, as Sasha got into the driver's seat of the SUV and restarted the engine.

Thirty Three

'We're here,' Sasha announced, turning to face Freya and smiling at her.

They'd driven a little more than fifteen minutes, according to the clock on the dashboard. There had come off the main road and headed up what felt like a dirt track. Freya's hands were aching and the wire was cutting into the skin. She'd had to lie on her side to relieve the pressure but now she was stuck there.

Sasha got down out of the car and opened the back door. She grabbed Freya's arms and pulled her up into a sitting position.

'Get up, bitch. I said we're here.' Sasha pulled Freya down and out of the car.

She managed to land on her feet but smarted as the twine tightened on her wrists. She looked at her surroundings. They were next to a patch of wasteland that was instantly familiar.

'We're at County Bridge.'

She could see the black bridge just a hundred yards or so away. It was so cold. The wind was whipping underneath her jacket and her fingers were starting to numb.

'Yes, don't sound so surprised. I know how much you love this place. You've spent hours here taking photographs, all of them dull and boring by the way. But, it seemed a fitting place for it all to end. A last tribute if you like.'

'Look, Sasha, this is stupid. You don't hate me. You certainly don't want to kill me. Why don't we just talk about this like grown-ups?'

'You *are* kidding right? You think talking can resolve anything? Did I not make myself clear enough earlier? You have my man. You are standing in the way of our happiness together. The only resolution to this is for you to be gone...completely gone.'

Sasha was becoming more and more unstable from what Freya could remember about captor behaviour. She only had her vast Bruce Willis and Arnold Schwarzenegger DVD collection to reference from but it wasn't looking good. She was really scared. What if Sasha was really going to try and kill her? It sounded completely far-fetched but the look in the woman's eyes told Freya this wasn't some sort of prank. Sasha was serious.

Sasha reached into her bag and drew out a white piece of cloth. She started to toy with it in her hands.

'What are you going to do?' Freya asked.

'You'll see. Come on, there's not much time.'

Sasha pushed Freya forward and jabbed the gun into the small of her back, urging her on towards the bridge.

Freya looked at the landscape in front of her. It was just grassland, the old ruined church and nothing else. Just wild open space and not another soul in sight. She had a thought. The fishermen! There must be some fishermen a little further up the river. She could shout or make a run for it or something. She had to do *something*.

'In case you're thinking about making a run for it, let me tell you…there's no one round here. You told me exactly what time the fishermen arrive and leave, remember? Anyway, I have no doubt I could out run you and we all know a bullet can travel a hell of a lot faster than both of us.'

'Sasha, this is insane. You can't possibly think you can kill me and get away with it.'

'Yoo hoo! I'm the one holding all the cards here! Oh *and* the gun. I think I have the upper hand. I think I'm more likely to get away with doing it than you're likely to get away from me.'

'And when I'm dead? When Nick's baby is dead. What then?'

'I told you. He'll be a little saddened, for a while. Then I will be there to pick up the pieces and step into your shoes.'

'You sad bitch. You really believe that, don't you?! You're warped!'

Bang! The gun went off and Freya screamed out loud, closing her eyes in anticipation of pain. Pain didn't come and she turned around to face Sasha. The woman was stood, looking furious, the gun pointed to the sky.

'If you make one more comment like that…one more…I swear to God I'll blow you away.'

Sasha's teeth were bared, her expression wild and Freya's heart sank to the floor. How was she going to get out of this one?

'Get on the bridge,' Sasha ordered, turning Freya back around and pushing her shoulder roughly.

Tears running down her face, Freya reluctantly stepped onto the bridge and began to walk along it. She had never felt so terrified and all she could think of was Nicholas and their baby. The baby she hadn't really wanted, hadn't been planning for. The baby she now so desperately longed to protect.

'So, what do you really know about these bridges, Freya?' Sasha asked as she followed her across the wooden slats.

'I...they were built by the Christian Fathers so people could get across the river to the churches in the area,' Freya spoke quickly, trying to compose herself.

'That's right, they were. You see, since you seem to have made these bridges something of a muse, I thought I would look into what fascinated you about them.'

'I just think the designs are wonderful and the rural location makes them even more spectacular.'

Her lips were dry and the cold, winter wind was sucking the moisture from them as they walked. The clouds were even darker out here than in Mayleaf. There was a storm brewing.

'Hmm, as I thought. You don't really know anything about what happened here.'

'Something happened here? What, like an important event?' Freya inquired.

'It was important to a lot of people at the time, yes. Stop!' Sasha ordered.

Freya shivered and did as she was told, coming to rest at the middle of the bridge.

'*Glory to the Father, leave sorrow behind and take hope from the past*,' Sasha spoke as she came up beside Freya and ran her fingers across the inscription on the side of the bridge.

'You know what that means?' Freya asked through chattering teeth.

'Oh yes, I know what it means. And you're going to find out exactly what it means.'

Sasha produced the white cloth she'd been holding earlier. Before Freya had a chance to react, she pulled it across Freya's face as a blindfold. She tied it tightly around the back of her head and Freya was then unable to see.

'Sasha, please. Don't do this. There's still a chance to stop all this. We'll forget about everything, no charges for anything. Just let me go,' Freya pleaded.

She was completely disorientated. She couldn't see anything through the cloth at all. She felt sick and dizzy and her heart galloped.

'Let's duck underneath these railings and see if we can smell the water,' Sasha suggested.

She pushed Freya underneath the rails, holding her by her bound wrists.

Freya let out a cry and held her breath, unable to get her bearings. She felt off-kilter, unable to balance.

'The Christian Fathers were all a bit mad, Freya. Oh they were all very charity driven, a bit like you. But they didn't like change. They didn't like revolution, or growth of knowledge, or advances in the world. They built themselves a commune. A town within a town. They barred themselves from the outside world. But, one day, after months of meetings and deliberations, the authorities took it upon themselves to break into the commune and threaten its existence. The law couldn't allow people to live against their rules, creating different values from the ones everyone else adhered to. They were warned, they were told they had to integrate,' Sasha explained.

'What happened?'

If she kept her talking it would buy time and she could get a feel for her position on the bridge. She had to try and stay calm.

'What happened? Well, the Christian Fathers just couldn't live the way the rest of us do. After all, they believed we were all on the path to hell and damnation. So, they all congregated. All nine hundred of them, on this very bridge. They all dressed in black, all wearing white blindfolds. And, holding hands and muttering prayers under their breath, they all just…jumped. Just like that. A whole line of nine hundred people just jumped into the water.' She loosened her grip of Freya, making her fall forward.

Freya screamed. Sasha tightened her grip, holding on to her again.

'And then there was nothing. No fighting for air. No flailing around in the water or struggling for breath. Just the sound of the crows overhead. Get the connection now? I thought it was fitting. I gave you a little insight into your demise,' Sasha spoke, putting her mouth right up close to Freya's ear.

'Miss Kelly! This is the LAPD! Drop your weapon!'

The sound of a voice through a loud hailer startled both the women. Sasha held Freya tighter and pushed the barrel of the gun hard against her temple.

'You're wasting your time, officers! I don't care what you're planning to do to me. She dies now!' Sasha screamed.

Freya could feel her heart beating hard against her chest. She couldn't see anything but the white of the blindfold. The arrival of the authorities was doing nothing to quell her anxiety. They weren't on the bridge. Anything could happen.

'Sasha, come on. What's going on?' Nicholas yelled.

Sasha turned her head. Nicholas was at the end of the bridge, in front of the police. He began slowly walking towards them.

'Nick,' Sasha greeted in a soft voice.

'What are you doing here? What are you doing with Freya?'

'I'm getting rid of her, Nick. For us. So we can be together. Oh, I've wanted to tell you so many times but it was never right. Something, or should I say, *someone* always got in the way.'

'Sasha, let Freya go.'

'I will. I'm going to…right into the river, just like the Christian Fathers. She loves these bridges. It's only fair she gets an ending she deserves,' Sasha replied.

Freya felt Sasha's fingers loosen and she slipped forward again.

'I love you, Nick,' Freya called.

Tears were streaming down her face now as the reality of what has about to happen hit her.

'Shut up, bitch!' She released the safety catch on the gun.

'Sasha, this is crazy. Come on, you don't need to do this for us. Just let her go.' He inched closer to them.

'I have to do this. She will always get in the way. And now there's a brat too. It will ruin everything.'

'No it won't. I promise it won't. Just let Freya go and we can talk about this…together,' Nicholas assured her.

Freya could feel herself starting to hyperventilate. Her chest was straining from being held in a bent position and she didn't know how long she could stay that way without having to move. But she couldn't move. Sasha had hold of her arms, her wrists were tied and not being able to see was making the panic build.

'You don't mean that. It's too soon. I'm not stupid. You would need time. That was the plan. I would get rid of her and give you some space and then you would realise it was all for the best. It can't happen yet,' Sasha said, shaking her head.

'I don't need time, Sasha. I just need you to trust me. You trust me, don't you?' He leveled a smile at her, gaining more ground.

'Of course I trust you. I love you, Nick.' She smiled back at him.

Freya was crying hard now, unable to stop herself. The pain of the position she was in and the emotion of having to listen to Sasha's declarations was overwhelming her.

'Then if you love me, give me the gun and let go of Freya. None of this is important. You're the special one, Sasha. We need to find a way to go forward from here.'

Sasha nodded and took the gun away from Freya's head.

'Give the gun to me,' Nicholas ordered.

Sasha held the gun out to Nicholas and he took it. He disarmed it and held it above his head.

'I've got the gun,' he called.

With that said, the police began to swarm onto the bridge.

'Why are they coming onto the bridge? Get back! Get back all of you!' Sasha yelled, her expression manic. She loosened her grip on Freya again, lowering her out and over the water.

'Sasha, don't be stupid. Let Freya go. I said we'll talk about this.'

Freya let out a scream. She felt like she was hanging on.

'You don't love me, do you? You still love her. I can see it in your eyes. I can see the fear and the love and the pitiful emotion. You don't care for me at all,' Sasha said, her breathing erratic and her hands shaking.

'That isn't true, Sasha. I do care.'

'What are you doing here? What are you doing with Freya?'

'I'm getting rid of her, Nick. For us. So we can be together. Oh, I've wanted to tell you so many times but it was never right. Something, or should I say, *someone* always got in the way.'

'Sasha, let Freya go.'

'I will. I'm going to...right into the river, just like the Christian Fathers. She loves these bridges. It's only fair she gets an ending she deserves,' Sasha replied.

Freya felt Sasha's fingers loosen and she slipped forward again.

'I love you, Nick,' Freya called.

Tears were streaming down her face now as the reality of what has about to happen hit her.

'Shut up, bitch!' She released the safety catch on the gun.

'Sasha, this is crazy. Come on, you don't need to do this for us. Just let her go.' He inched closer to them.

'I have to do this. She will always get in the way. And now there's a brat too. It will ruin everything.'

'No it won't. I promise it won't. Just let Freya go and we can talk about this...together,' Nicholas assured her.

Freya could feel herself starting to hyperventilate. Her chest was straining from being held in a bent position and she didn't know how long she could stay that way without having to move. But she couldn't move. Sasha had hold of her arms, her wrists were tied and not being able to see was making the panic build.

'You don't mean that. It's too soon. I'm not stupid. You would need time. That was the plan. I would get rid of her and give you some space and then you would realise it was all for the best. It can't happen yet,' Sasha said, shaking her head.

'I don't need time, Sasha. I just need you to trust me. You trust me, don't you?' He leveled a smile at her, gaining more ground.

'Of course I trust you. I love you, Nick.' She smiled back at him.

Freya was crying hard now, unable to stop herself. The pain of the position she was in and the emotion of having to listen to Sasha's declarations was overwhelming her.

'Then if you love me, give me the gun and let go of Freya. None of this is important. You're the special one, Sasha. We need to find a way to go forward from here.'

Sasha nodded and took the gun away from Freya's head.

'Give the gun to me,' Nicholas ordered.

Sasha held the gun out to Nicholas and he took it. He disarmed it and held it above his head.

'I've got the gun,' he called.

With that said, the police began to swarm onto the bridge.

'Why are they coming onto the bridge? Get back! Get back all of you!' Sasha yelled, her expression manic. She loosened her grip on Freya again, lowering her out and over the water.

'Sasha, don't be stupid. Let Freya go. I said we'll talk about this.'

Freya let out a scream. She felt like she was hanging on.

'You don't love me, do you? You still love her. I can see it in your eyes. I can see the fear and the love and the pitiful emotion. You don't care for me at all,' Sasha said, her breathing erratic and her hands shaking.

'That isn't true, Sasha. I do care.'

Nicholas put his hand out in an attempt to grab hold of Sasha but she stepped back away from him.

'Not enough,' she replied through gritted teeth.

She let go of Freya and sent her plunging from the bridge into the murky water below.

'Oh my God! What have you done? Freya!'

He looked down into the river, as he pulled off his shoes. Then, ducking under the railings, he dived down into the water.

'Miss Kelly, you are under arrest. Tell her the details, Barney. And get some people down there or we're going to be headline news for all the wrong reasons. I don't want drownings on my watch,' the female officer said, cuffing Sasha.

Nicholas bobbed up from the dive and searched around for Freya, hoping she'd surfaced. There was no sign of her. He dived down under the water again. It was so dull and dirty, the visibility was practically non-existent. He came up for breath and filled his lungs. He desperately wiped at his eyes to clear the dirt from them and looked over at the bank.

Clinging to the dirt at the edge of the river, with one hand, mud all over her face and the blindfold around her neck was Freya. She was breathing heavily, she looked weak, but she was alive.

Police officers were just coming down the bank to assist them and Nicholas swam across the river to reach her.

'Freya, oh God. Come on, let's get you out of here,' he said, putting his arms around her and bringing her closer to where their rescuers were starting to congregate.

'My other hand...it's still tied. I couldn't get it loose. I...' Freya said.

She was freezing. She felt like a human Popsicle. Everything was numb.

'It's OK. You're going to be OK. I promise, it's all over now,' Nicholas reassured. He grabbed hold of the bank and tried to help Freya from the water.

'What about...the baby...do you think...' Freya began.

A police officer helped Nicholas pull Freya up from the water.

'The most important thing is you, Freya.'

'I know how much you wanted this baby, Nick. I really wanted it too.'

Her head was muzzy and breathing was a struggle. She fought to remain conscious.

'Everything's going to be fine, Freya. I promise.'

'Do you think it's going to snow?' she asked as the paramedic team hurried towards them.

Thirty Four

Crows filled her head. Crows, dirty water and people dressed in black. Their faces were hidden and they were leaping into the water, scores at a time.

Freya snapped open her eyes and took in her surroundings. It was familiar. It was her and Nicholas' bedroom. It was home. She was filled with relief.

Willis climbed up onto her and pressed his cold, wet nose into her cheek.

'Hey, boy,' Freya said, stroking his fur as he turned around and around in circles.

Everything hurt. It had been almost a week and everything still hurt. Just breathing made her chest ache and she had been confined to the bedroom, by order of Dr. Stone. She was sick of it. She hated being dependent on Nicholas to look after her. It was driving her crazy and, as sweet as it was he was seeing to her every need, what she really wanted to do was get up and get back to being the one who gave the orders.

On the bedside cabinet was a plate of fish, potato and green vegetables Nicholas had made her for lunch. She hadn't been able to touch it. Just looking at the food made her feel sick. Even though her stomach was empty.

Her empty stomach. It growled on cue, as if to let her know it hadn't been satisfied. Freya placed her hand under the duvet and smoothed the skin with her hand.

Her abdomen wasn't entirely empty. There was still a baby growing inside her and he or she was probably hungry too. Perhaps it was time to give healthy food a try.

She looked over at the plate and nausea rose in her throat. Before she had the chance to think anymore about eating it, the phone rang.

She snatched it up before Nicholas answered from downstairs.

'Hello.'

'And how is the patient doing today?' Emma asked her.

'Oh, Em, it's great to hear your voice.'

'How are you feeling? I rang late last night. Nick said you were asleep and I didn't want to disturb you.'

'I've been doing a lot of sleeping. If I sleep it means Nick has less time to keep on about me seeing a therapist to get over the trauma. I mean, which trauma does he want me to talk to them about? I could be having two hour sessions twice a week for the rest of my life and it still might not be enough.'

'He's so worried about you, Freya. You and the baby. He just wants to do what's best.'

'I know. But can you imagine what a field day any therapist would have with me? I can't go there. I don't need to go there.'

'None of this is your fault. You have to keep focused on that. You've been let down by most of the people in your life. They've done that to you because of who *they* are.'

'I know how to pick them, don't I?'

'Well, you can't choose your family and as for Sasha…well it sounds like she did a very good job of being believable.'

'Yes, she did.'

'So, I suppose you aren't really feeling up to a wedding at the moment. Have you rearranged the date?'

'No, not yet. There's been so much going on there hasn't been a chance and we really want to do it properly.'

'Oh well, I was hoping I hadn't wasted a trip.'

'What?'

'I stopped by that Chinese you keep telling me about. I just had to see in real life. I got sweet and sour chicken balls, egg foo yung and beef in black bean sauce if you're hungry.'

The bedroom door opened and Emma appeared, a phone to her ear and a takeaway bag in her hand.

Freya screamed. She leapt out of bed, sending Willis crashing to the floor and enveloped her friend in a bear hug.

'Careful! Don't do yourself an injury or Nick will never forgive me,' Emma exclaimed, hugging her friend tightly.

'I can't believe you're here! This is the best thing! You came all the way from Corfu? All ten hours and…'

'And a stop in Paris,' Emma replied, smiling.

Tears were pricking Freya's eyes as she looked at her best friend. It was so good to see her. She needed her.

'It's so good to see you and I love your hair that colour,' Emma said.

'It's good to see you too. So, where's Melly and Yiannis? They'd better be here.'

'They certainly are. They're downstairs with Nick.'

'Nick knew, didn't he? He knew you were planning to come over.'

'How could I not come, Freya? After what happened to you I wanted to come straight away. Nick called me and told me everything and then it was all over the television and in the papers. But he said you needed some time. So we waited until he said you were feeling better. He arranged our flights and here we are.'

'I'm starting to worry about his knack for concealing things from me,' Freya stated.

'I told him not to tell you because I knew you'd try to talk me out of coming all this way with Melly. And I wanted to come. I wanted to see you and your beautiful house and Willis. I think I caught a glimpse of him a second ago. I wanted to see your town and all the people you've described to me.'

'Would you believe Brian quite possibly saved my life?'

'Would you believe he's selling t-shirts with "Baby Kaden says Go Maulers Go" printed on them?' Emma asked her.

'Actually, yes.'

'I guess that's what you'd call a "Brian Episode".'

'You're getting into the Mayleaf way.'

'So, do you want some of this Chinese food? Or have you already eaten?' She indicated the plate of food on the nightstand.

'*That* stuff? Get real! I'm coming down.' She picked up her robe and wrapped around her.

'Are you allowed out of bed? Perhaps we should check with Nick first.'

'You *are* joking, right? I need to start reminding him who wears the trousers in this relationship.'

When the two women arrived in the kitchen, Nicholas was holding Melissa in his arms and feeding her a bottle of milk.

'Aw, would you look at that? He's a natural,' Emma said.

'Hi, Yiannis, it's great to see you,' Freya said, kissing the Greek man on the cheek.

'And to see you too,' Yiannis responded, hugging her.

'I thought you were breastfeeding, Em,' Freya said. She stood next to Nicholas and looked down at the very contented Melissa.

'I was. All I will say is "puncture wounds".' Emma pulled a face.

'Bottles and teats. Add it to our list,' Freya said, directing it at Nicholas.

'Added. Hey, what are you doing out of bed?' he asked her.

'You used to say that to me so often when we first got together. It's nice romance is still such a big part of our relationship.'

'Feeling better?' Nicholas asked.

'Much better now Emma's here with Chinese food. Em, the plates are in the cupboard over there,' Freya directed.

'By the way, this package arrived for you earlier. It's from Josie. She said she found them while she was cat-sitting and we were at the hospital. She said something about Willis scratching around the back of the sofa and then she said she'd laundered them. Does any of that make any sense to you?' Nicholas asked her. He indicated a brown paper bag on the countertop.

'Not a bit. Let's see...Oh! How embarrassing!' Freya exclaimed, looking into the bag.

'What is it?' Emma asked.

'Remember those undergarments I told you went missing. The ones I was sure would end up on EBay.'

'Wild Wednesday?'

'Wild Wednesday! I can't believe one of my neighbours has had to handle a pair of my pants.'

Nicholas laughed and Yiannis looked completely bemused.

'Come on, Yiannis, help me serve up this food,' Emma said, taking plates to the breakfast bar.

'Melly's beautiful isn't she?' Nicholas remarked to Freya.

Freya put her little finger into the tiny hand of the baby and smiled as Melissa tightened her grip around it.

'Yes she is. She has her mother's good looks and her father's brooding Greek eyes.'

'I wonder what our baby's going to look like.'

'Hopefully he or she will have their father's good looks and restraint when it comes to food and their mother's dynamic wit and sparkling personality.'

'And lots of health and happiness,' Nicholas added.

'And some normality. Please, God, a shed load of normality,' Freya begged.

'Let's toast that thought with one of Bruce's chicken balls,' Nicholas suggested.

'One? I've been out of proper eating action for a week. I hope Emma ordered big.'